SOME RECOLLECTIONS OF ST. IVES

Also by David Mamet

SOME RECOLLECTIONS OF ST. IVES

THE MEMOIRS OF CHARLES HOLLIS

First published in 1965, here presented with previously
unpublished material; annotated and with an introduction
and afterword by George Choate.

DAVID MAMET

Arcade Publishing • New York

Arcade Publishing books may be purchased in bulk at special discounts for sales promotion, corporate gifts, fund-raising, or educational purposes. Special editions can also be created to specifications. For details, contact the Special Sales Department, Arcade Publishing, 307 West 36th Street, 11th Floor, New York, NY 10018 or arcade@ skyhorsepublishing.com.

Arcade Publishing® is a registered trademark of Skyhorse Publishing, Inc.®, a Delaware corporation.

Visit our website at www.arcadepub.com.

Please follow our publisher Tony Lyons on Instagram @tonylyonsisuncertain.

10 9 8 7 6 5 4 3 2 1

Library of Congress Cataloging-in-Publication Data is available on file.

Cover design by David Ter-Avanesyan
Cover image from the George Grantham Bain Collection

Print ISBN: 978-1-64821-140-9
Ebook ISBN: 978-1-64821-141-6

Printed in the United States of America

SOME RECOLLECTIONS OF ST. IVES

INTRODUCTION
To the 2025 Edition

Charles Hollis was a student at the St. Ives School, 1894–1898.

At the outbreak of World War I he left the United States and enlisted in the British Army, Welsh Guards, and served, throughout 1914–1916.

Seriously wounded at the Battle of Loos, he was invalided to London, where he spent most of the ensuing two years in treatment at Guys Hospital. He there met Artemis Ross-Merry, a nurse.[1]

They married in 1918, on his discharge.

Hollis spent the next two years at Oxford, studying English Literature under John Fraser-Ward.

In 1921 he and Mrs. Hollis returned to the States.

The following year he was engaged by Edward Fossett, then Head, to teach at St. Ives.

He served, as probationary instructor, teacher, House Master, and was, in 1939, appointed Headmaster, in which position he served until his retirement in 1965.

After his retirement he remained active in School life. He and his wife lived at The Willows, the cottage they bought on his return

---

[1] She was the daughter of Patricia and Harold Ross-Merry. He achieved fame as a contributor to (later, editor of), the English Hunting Journal, *The Field*, as the creator of the comic "Master of the Fox Hounds" *Colonel Rosemary*. Drawings, by SPY, in both *The Field* and *Punch* can be seen, to this day, in the Green Room of the Field House.

to St. Ives. It was purchased by the school in 1971 and, since then it has served as the school's "Guest Quarters."

Hollis served for many years on the Board of Governors, and as Editor Emeritus of *The Sentinel*.

He was a frequent contributor to *The New England Journal of Private Education*, the British *Education*, and the French, *L'Academie*.

The couple had one child, Patricia (Pet).

An army nurse, she served with distinction in the South Pacific. After her death, Hollis became active in Veterans Affairs—an activity he maintained throughout his life.

His wife Artemis died in 1958. After her death he began these memoirs (the only book he would publish). He died in 1968, and is buried next to his wife, on the Hill.

Hollis was (few knew) the recipient of both the British Distinguished Service Order and the French Croix de Guerre. He refused all other honors.

As headmaster Hollis was often erroneously addressed as "Doctor." He, in fact, possessed no academic degrees, having left Oxford prior to sitting his Examinations.

On his return to the States, he applied to Fossett for a position teaching.

The Board had recently passed a ruling (rescinded in 1950, and reinstated three years later) that only those possessing a minimum of a bachelor's degree could be hired to teach at the School.

Fossett was profusely apologetic to Hollis, whom he had known as a student, and of whose love of English Literature he was well aware.

"I am devastated that I cannot, at this time, offer you the position," Fossett said.

They began to take their farewells, in the Hall. While putting on their coats, Fossett gestured to the school's two-horse shay, which brought Hollis from, and would now transport him back to, the Station.

"How was the ride?" he said.

"Slow, very slow," Hollis said. "The horses, God bless them, are so old."

"Yes," Fossett said, "one tires, and the other tires in sympathy. We call them Remedy and Grief."

"Of course," Hollis said, "when Remedy's exhausted, so is Grief."[2]

Fossett shook his head and removed Hollis's coat, and extemporized for him the position of Probationary Instructor in Grammar. He wrote the Board informing them of the appointment and said if they didn't like it they could have his resignation.

Hollis served as Fossett's Secretary; as teacher of English and History, then House Master; and, eventually, Head, a position for which we suspect Fossett had singled him out from the first.

During his Headmastership he was offered numerous Academic Honors and Degrees, all of which he, graciously, declined.[3]

Forty Years at St. Ives, written on his retirement, was intended as a Memento, for distribution within the School Community.

Many allusions, and much wit, intended for that readership and treasured by them, must be beyond those "not of the School."

This new edition contains notes for the benefit of a wider audience, and material included in the manuscript, but excised from the originally published version.

— George Choate, 2025

---

2   Note: *Othello*, Act One, Scene Three.

3   "I cannot reflect credit upon those institutions, never having studied there. They would hardly have honored me if I had, who was always a wretched student." HOLLIS, Personal Correspondence, 1922.

HOLLIS'S DEDICATION:

To the memory of Temmy and of Pet

St. Mihiel, 1914
("The St. Ives Hymn")

They must be pitied who have not seen
Chapel and Hall and the path between
The steeples sharp in the Autumn air
The hurrying friends on the Library stair.
They in their poverty have not been heard
The boisterous song at the tavern Board
The Tower Clock tell its ancient word
To the men on the Darkening Green.

The years can ne'er restore our Brief College Days
Comfort or soothe our sorrow oe'er the Parting Ways
But pledge we solemnly and witness the same
Honor and pride and joy beside, in our school name.

Now visions of study and sounds of play
Grow soft in the vanishing light of day
The faces of youth rise to my mind
I think of the friends I have left behind
How many in nature, how many in war
Have passed to the care of a farther shore
And I hear the sound of the Boatman's oar
And my spirit is moved to pray.

The years can ne'er restore our Brief College Days
Comfort or soothe our sorrow oe'er the Parting Ways
But pledge we solemnly and witness the same
Honor and pride and joy beside, in our school name.

—Anonymous

These Memoirs, friends have suggested, might as easily been titled "Fifty Years . . ."

I exempt my four Student years and the interregnum, of course, of the war years, my convalescence in England, and attendance at Oxford.

C. H.

OCCUPATION MARKS

I imagine my retirement as the life of an exile.

The Court-in-Exile has, over time, dwindled—its titles and ranks now understood as moot, as we admit the impossibility of return. For our country is no more. For our country is the Past. And so we are free, as individuals, to seek out philosophy, that solace fashioned of humility and sorrow. This may be, courteously, enjoyed only in solitude, removed from the temptations to garrulousness, for my descent toward which I hope I may be forgiven.

I planned to write a book of some possible interest to those who, even now, are just across the Green, the South Field, and Ferry Road. I see that they are not my readership, though they may someday be.

I hope that my devotion to my beloved topic may have spared the reader some (I cannot hope for All) of the solecisms attendant upon reminiscences.

I do not mean my depiction of the school's Heroic Age as an indictment of its current state, its Masters, or their understandings of the doctrines, inevitably, elaborated and new-understood or rejected, which they have received from their predecessors. Such indictments may, in the old, absorb (and to no point whatsoever) an energy otherwise devolving into the simple but sad avowal that it is not paths of glory alone which lead to the Grave.

Which of us, in his most secret heart, does not know himself to be both hypocrite and liar? One may positively avoid sanctimony only by remaining mute, but we are all marked by our trades. Mine has involved writing and speech.

~

The subject of Jellicoe's 1905 Closing Address (*The Serial*, #41) was *Occupation Marks*.

He had been made aware of the study by Henry Parge (St. Ives, 1889), who was, for a brief period in 1905, Assistant Police Commissioner of New York City—the first of that family whose traditional support of our School continues to this day.

Parge was the New Broom which sweeps clean—an outsider brought in to clean the Augean Stables of Tammany Hall. He became enamored of police work, his study of which lead to the publication of his *Occupation Marks Used in the Detection of Crime*.[4] It was dedicated to Jellicoe, "whose support and direction has always inspired me"; and, indeed, it was Jellicoe's comment which inspired him to write the book.

Visiting his son at school (Henry Parge II, St. Ives, 1910), Parge shared with the Doctor his fascination with the technical aspects of detection. The Head suggested he write a book. Parge replied he was not a writer. "As your career here suggested," Jellicoe said, "but, perhaps, you had not then found that of sufficient interest to focus your thoughts."

And, so Parge went on to write his book (and to two terms as Lieutenant Governor of Connecticut, inter alia), and the Head took from the conversation the theme of that year's Closing Address.

---

4   1906 Ed.

From *The Serial*:

The blacksmith may be discerned by his fire-seared forearms, the plowman by his cupped and calloused palms, still moulded to the handles. See also the furrowed brow and squint of the Editor, gone weak-sighted in his work; the hod carrier's raised right shoulder; the knife's callosity in the web of the chef's right hand.

We know also the development of various strengths of intellect, and their discernable effects, both for good and ill, upon the character, these no less deformations than the porter's bowed back.

Just as the policeman becomes, of necessity universally suspicious, so may the philosopher cultivate habits of thought so little leagued to conventional wisdom that they may conduce equally to insight or absurdity.

And what of the Educator? He inevitably comes to perceive lessons in all things, and, taxed over time, must forfeit the strength necessary to curtail their expression.

In which category (Educator) I now find myself, and for which progressed garrulousness I ask for your understanding, adducing Jellicoe, to plead the Habits of a Lifetime, which, in mine, as in any profession, mature into those necessary deformations we call habit. The habit forms the man.

I have spent my life as a teacher at the St. Ives School, and these are some of the things that I remember.

∽

"But not as in the days of my Youth," Fossett had written, in that reminiscence to which this must be, in large extent, an homage.[5]

5　"The School as I Knew It," G. Fossett, 1925, Privately Printed.

"Not as in the days of my youth"—as if anything ever retained that form.

Still, with him, as with others less self-aware, the bittersweet observation must have been a comfort. Things change, and those who age to recognize this as universal law do so with an organism whose decay must inspire an ascription of a similar progression to the World They Knew—that it, similarly, existed and exists in stasis only as a comforting fiction. The wistful phrases of dismissal of a modern life conceal not only the pride of status gained through primogeniture, but indictment of the viciously wasteful and unnecessary elaborations of one who must be God.

For why, we muse, must human beings age full of regret not only for those sins we have committed, but for those we have neglected to commit? "But it was not as in the days of my youth," the title originally chosen by Fossett's sister for the (posthumous) publication of that diary which, published as *Recollections*, would be distributed along with the Cap and the Red Blazer, to all incoming students, on their first day at School. It is found, to this day, on the shelves and in the Memento boxes of the notable, and it was discovered in the tunic pockets of those fallen both at the Somme and at Okinawa. It has been placed, at the decedent's request, in many a coffin, and copies have been passed to three, and, I am reminded now, to four generations.

An alumnus, shot down at the Yalu River, had used the pages of the book to stanch the wound which had brought him down. He recalls reading the chapter "Character and Myth," for solace, and using its last page "L'envoi" to roll a cigarette from that tobacco ruined by his spattered blood, washed by his canteen, and dried on a Korean rock. He wrote, in apology (*The Serial*, 1954), "I know Dr. Hollis would not have minded." James Boll ('48), US Navy, survived his downing, was rescued, and returned to combat.

After the War, he created that business for which he is remembered, and personally funded not only the New Buildings, but the complete restoration of The Hall, after the fire of 1961. His son, William (St. Ives, 1958) was the recipient of the school's Holland Prize, now renamed in his honor. He died over Vietnam in September, 1964.

It is he, we are told, who is depicted in George Archer Coopers, "Not Fallen," which image has, beneath the School's Crest, adorned the masthead every subsequent issue of *The Misfit*. This was not James Boll's only gift to the school, for it was, coincidentally, he who discovered, in his own father's diary, that folded sheet, the handwritten war poem, *St. Mihiel*, 1914, which, set to music, as the *St. Ives Hymn*, has been sung at every Commencement since its discovery.

Bill Holland's regiment was in the Salient previously occupied by the Scottish Borderers. It was there, according to his diary, that the poem was found, tacked to the headquarters trench wall. It has long been suggested that the unknown author must have been a Son of Eton, or another of those British schools from which Jellicoe and the early masters of St. Ives have unashamedly taken our model.

~

Historians delight in positing a progression, based upon military strength, political folly, and so on; biographers choose heredity or environment upon which to mold their work. Both, finally, are simply creating myths, the operative element in which, however rationally described, may be called Fate.

The Plains Indians considered history differently.

Each year they met for the Winter Count. The tribe would depict that year's signal events in drawings, and commemorate them in song, and the year, then, would be memorialized as that when the

Bison were scarce, or when the water turned bad, or the snow fell in June, and so on.

This, of course, is the way a family counts history.

And so I, acting here, similarly, must be recounting the history of a Family, or of a Tribe—the years marked, in my mind, by The Fire, the appearance, departure, or death of notable persons; the crimes and scandals, extraordinary occasions of service or cowardice, occasions of humor or wisdom.

Finally, they are the Winter Count, and, perhaps, something like that mythic experience of the drowning man. But it is not his "life" which passes before his eyes, but memories, their order and appearance adding, if not a last insight, then a closing oddity to his **life**.

THE FIRE[6]

The financial loss to the school had been called "immeasurable," by those great Eastern Publications, many of which had sheltered or nourished our graduates during the days of their first employment, a progression and tradition, it seems, still observed by the "ink-fingered grinds" of *The Misfit*—its writers and editors passing into the care and tutelage of their elder brother.

This institutional nepotism might be correctly called "charity" were it not for the appearance, in our graduates, advanced into the journalistic ranks, of some talent; and, of course, once, we may say, of genius.

The reputation of Frank Whitton (St. Ives, 1912–1916) has always been linked with that of the School. The marriage has not always been a happy one. The publication of his *The Harrow and the Field* (1935) occasioned in the Alumni a vehemence near-incomprehensible today.

The press, of course, received it as a *roman a clef*, and, as such, an unassailable indictment of life at the School. Parents called for the removal not only of this, but of all of Whitton's works from the school library, and even (yes) for the excision of his name from the plaque on the Office Door, listing *The Misfit's* editors.

This request was, politely, denied by the Proctor, a position, then, as now, vexed with all requests comfortably shunned by other authority. He (Danner Davis Bane, St. Ives, 1929) replied to each

---

6   March 5, 1961, Ed.

of the parents subscribing to the Petition, that, if they felt the time came to remove from our library those volumes offensive to some sensibilities, the offended were welcome to ΜΩΛΩΝ ΛΑΒΕ. Writing in that Greek with which the Spartans responded to the Persians' request, at Thermopylae, to "lay down your arms," their response, "Come and take them."

That he wrote in Greek was, he later wrote, not an assertion of intellectual superiority, "any child can learn Greek," nor an indictment to the parents who were, of course, ignorant of that classic tongue, but, rather, "for the style of the Thing" (Danner Bane, *Memoirs*, St. Ives Library).

The Parents, the Alumni, and the Board were, it is not too strong a word, stunned by Whitton's book, but the Faculty, curiously, took it in stride.

I say "curiously" as a lifetime acquaintance with schoolmasters has failed to blunt my wonder at their pathological conservatism.

I believe they were, if not emboldened, then inspired by the bravery of the Proctor, "taking pride in his strength, rather than refuge in their fear" (James Hemmings, Eulogy for Donald Davis Bane, 1971).

We note that the tradition of adding the name of each editor of *The Misfit* to the office door has continued to this day. The list, dating from 1871, now occupies also the adjacent wall. And there is the one name missing, that of Frank Whitton, defaced by an act of vandalism—the culprit never identified—in 1935, upon publication of the book.

That space, and the eradication of his name, have been, since then, the first thing a New Boy is shown on his arrival of the school. Since 1935, it has been the privilege of the current Editor to meet the new arrival, and to walk the Grounds with him. But the tour always begins at the newspaper office.

The Library, of course, burned in 1961. It has been rebuilt and refurbished through the great generosity of alumni. The Library Annex, and its collection of Rare Books, and, notably, of those first editions signed and dated by our Distinguished Alumni Authors was, of course, obliterated—though the Library now houses works so-created since that date, and a replacement of the lost volumes (though, of course, many unsigned, and none dedicated to the School).

The major donor to this effort of replacement is a name perhaps known to a few, and suspected by many, mention of which his bequest specifically prohibits.

He had suggested naming the Library in memory of Frank Whitton. The benefactor's request was, most generously, withdrawn when a canvas of the student body revealed an almost universal preference for the commemoration of Danner Davis Bane. The tone was set by an unsigned letter to *The Misfit* (February, 1961, "It is Burned"), "few can have talent, and few find fame, but anyone can be brave." *Soit.*

What of *The Harrow and the Field*?

Its suggestions of various crimes and abuses are today seen as tame, if not, indeed, as unworthy of note. The advent of "psychological criticism," which swept the Thirties, has "identified" a strain of sadism in the work and located it not in the school which the book supposedly portrays, but in the mind of the writer.

Well, what work cannot be understood thusly? The shield of the philistine is not individual probity, but the assertion of membership in the Moral group. Whitton stood and stands alone. Mather (St. Ives, 1959) wrote, of him, in *Theory and Application*:

If there is such a thing as Reality it most certainly is warped by perception, for no two human beings appreciate the same phenomenon in the same way. And even so-called irreducible scientific facts have been doubted, investigated and discarded by ensuing generations—else of what can science consist?

These perceptions are again reshaped, by the Artist into *new* phenomena, themselves inviting perception and, again, inseparable from inevitable interpretation and misunderstanding, allowing the process to begin again.

We note not only that a portrait is not a photograph, but that even a photograph may only be accepted as an accurate rendition of "reality" through the application of the thought processes so engrained as to have become unnoticeable, and, so, unknown to the viewer (the reduction of the subject to two dimensions, its altered size and coloration, and so on).

The painted portrait does similarly, and, for the supposed accuracy of the photograph's depiction, offers, instead, the possibility of deeper understanding.

Who has not experienced the initial rejection of a portrait, followed, on repeated viewing, of its revelation if not of some deeper truth then of an intriguing connection between the work of the artist and some ineffable aspect of the subject?

∾

The readers will note, in the digression above a certain reluctance to address the basic and troubling question as regards Whitton and *The Harrow*. I will not attempt to balance a perhaps understandable delicacy of approach against an unworthy hypocrisy. The book is, of course, a *roman à clef*. The facts of the case are known, the identity of the actors long-established. The book deserves all praise as a work of art, the surest accolade that it has never been and never will be out-of-print. The amends which any institution must make for its own infirmities—and what institution of any age is found without them—were made, in our case, prior to and thus not motivated by the publication of the novel; both Whitton and the Regents dealing, each in their own way, with the situation.

Changes in our school organization were instituted immediately upon the revelation of the crime, and remain in place and most stringently observed to this day.

All human beings are fragile. Some are evil. And good people may sin. Those are the lessons, imparted by the book, as lessons sometimes must be, by shock. The most important lesson, for the young, is to admit fault, and then to amend it.

Language, mathematics, and history may be learned, and more easily learned, from a book than in a classroom.

The formation of character has always been the essential purpose of our school.

The New Boy is given his blazer and cap, and taken to the *Misfit* office. His docent (always a member of TOP) will say, "On Saturday you'll be invited to the Head's for tea. He'll ask you what name was missing on the door, and to explain to him the difference between Civil Disobedience and Vandalism."

The new arrival, then, is from the first immersed in the culture of the school; his introduction, in the words of Dr. Jellicoe, much like that of the new recruit. "That which might appear as hazing may, on his matriculation, be recognized as, in fact, a blunt but sincere welcome to his new Society."

My predecessor, Dr. Fossett, wrote[7] of the observations of his contemporaries (Linguists Paula and Simon Starr), that the lore of children is unique. It is passed, from one generation to the next, through hundreds of years, seamlessly, without the interaction of adults. The children teach the children.

But Dr. Jellicoe knew, as we all know who have served in uniform, that this autonomic unmediated transmission is also found,

---

7   Private Diaries, 1931, Ed.

in the ranks, in the Military, "It is the treasure," he wrote,[8] "of the Ranks, who are the soul and essence of the Army."

He observed that officers are debarred from participation in this culture. They have been indoctrinated at the various Service Schools and Academies and are, thus, exempted from that education and trauma which is the possession of the subordinate culture, "which has undergone Ordeal."

In the Doctor's *Biography*, see the chapter "In the Shenandoah." Here he refers at length of the first days of his enlistment, the rigors of the march and bivouac, and "the unutterable joy of finding one belonged." He alludes to an anecdote he heard, on his first day, from a Sergeant who had fought in Mexico.

It does not appear in his Appendix, where we are bid seek it, (for reasons we can only conjecture, though it most likely may be put down to a Printer's Error), but it is alluded to in his ped-agogical writings, most especially in *The Calm Ordeal* (1889). [So-named, in the *Anthology*, but originally titled (*The Serial* 1880) *The Boy's First Day*.]

We learn that it was the Head's practice, in the school's first years, to meet the new arrival at the Gates (the job, since modern times, that of the First Seniors, in TOP), and walk him over the grounds, "Bumping the Bounds," a phrase and a practice which would have been familiar to any nineteenth-century person with the least acquaintance with rural life.

This was the Farmer's transmission, from father to son, of the knowledge of the extent of the family's land. The young boy would be led around the Farm's perimeter, and at each relevant landmark— the Old Stile, the third apple tree, the break in the Stone Wall, and so on, the boy would be roughly pushed into the marker.

---

8   Op cit.

So, Dr. Jellicoe wrote, is the transmission of any culture. It is not indoctrination, nor actually Education (meaning "learning"), but a third and more important thing, which is putting the child in a position *and a frame of mind* (Italics in the original) not to learn, but to *have* learned, "this is how we do things here."

"Here," to the Doctor, could be, and, indeed was, St. Ives, the United States of America, and Christianity, as practiced by—but not strictly limited to—the Episcopal Church.

At the outbreak of the Civil War, Jellicoe had enlisted in the 3rd Massachusetts as a Private, and had served with distinction until the Second Battle of the Wilderness. There, and now a Full Colonel, he had been grievously wounded by a Minié ball. He would be confined to the Military Hospital at Bethesda, Maryland for fourteen months.

He returned to the village in 1866, his body twisted, able to walk only with the aid of two canes. The house was empty, his parents having both died during the War. The Farm, under the care of the Welds, continued to "run itself."

There had never been, in his family, want, nor the fear of want, since the first Jellicoe had established his workshop (later the Factory) on the Connecticut River in 1755. The introduction of steam power had occasioned the removal of the factory to Marshfield, closer to Boston, and its shipping. The Farm, long the family's Summer Retreat, remained.

His great friend, Taylor Hobbs, had died at Chancellorsville, leaving a young widow and her two sons. She had "fallen into straightened circumstances"; and Jellicoe suggested she and the boys take the River House (today's Boat House) and do him the favor of keeping it inhabited. (During the days of waterpower it had been the lodging of the Head Mechanic of the Lock and Waterwheel.)

Mrs. Hobbs demurred, saying she would take the boys to Boston, as there was no school in St. Ives, and she did not consider herself sufficiently learned to instruct them, and knew herself too poor to afford a tutor. Jellicoe suggested she bring the boys to him and allow him to "try whether or not he might teach them something," and that was, of course, the beginning of our school.

The Village universally assumed the two would marry, but it was not to be; the reasons for which are beyond surmise. Mrs. Hobbs stayed in the River House until her marriage with Judge Brant. They and Dr. Jellicoe remained the closest of friends. The Doctor's dinner table, his workbench, the various mismatched chairs in the tack room, these became the two boy's "school." Their number was swelled, as now this and now that neighbor suggested that perhaps there might be room in the establishment for "one more boy."

The Doctor told Harry Forbes, the School's first Proctor (1898–1905), that, to him, the happiest phrase was that of the parent depositing his or her child at school with "I can't do a thing with him."

So the school grew, and both institutional success and error solidified into tradition.

Its reputation spread. The Jellicoe Fortune supported it, "Not as a charitable institution," the Doctor said, "but I will consider this money as the porch which kept the Stoics out of the weather, and so allowed them to continue their disputes in some comfort."

It is true that the School has had more than its share of military men, many passing from St. Ives to the Service Academies (including, in four cases, Sandhurst, and in two St. Cyr). For though the Doctor most certainly communicated his love of history and his understanding that the subject was the record of conflict—armed or financial—he also communicated his utter loathing of war, of which he had seen as much as any man of his time.

The students then, and we may hope, now, still, were exposed to the love of service, which perhaps led many of them into the Defense of their Country, as it led others into medicine and the Law.

St. Ives has produced (or as the Doctor was wont to say, "was privileged to have known") men of Letters, explorers, few scientists, and, as any institution—human nature being what it is—the odd criminal.

During his tenure, the Doctor was invited, by two recipients, to attend the award of the Medal of Honor; and, by the Condemned, to visit the Death Cell. This latter not on one occasion, as recorded, but in fact on two—the circumstances of the second to be revealed only on that still-far-off date specified in the Doctor's will, to be opened on the 50th anniversary of his death. The sealed document was lost, however in the fire of 1961, and the name of the condemned criminal, though widely conjectured, never known.

OF THE INSCRIPTIONS IN HALL

It is not, Halliwell taught, that we have no clear conception of Virtue. The Christian model of charity, understanding, patience and generosity is before us constantly—engraved in our hearts as a beloved, temporal fantasy.

> This figure is not Christ, but the imaginary being whose friendship and support, perfect in all things, we believe to be our desert, and whose absence we decry as our misfortune.
>
> Where is the proctor, teacher, philanthropist, friend who would give, unstintingly, of all that he had, happy to be repaid only by the joy of giving?
>
> This man so rich he could relieve my distress, that one so powerful he could elevate my talents to their just position; one so surpassingly just and persuasive who could banish the legal miseries into which I've fallen, another so courageous as to stand alone, in my defense, against the Mob.
>
> (Halliwell, in his *Valedictory to St. Ives*, 1925)

Retired and returned to England, he was recalled, at the age of eighty-three, as Temporary Head of Christchurch, on the death of Crawford, in the early days of The Blitz.

The 1925 ceremony of his retirement was attended by well over one thousand of the Alumni, the tent past overflowing full of the Old Boys; those of most recent date, their elders, survivors of The Great War, *their* predecessors, and men of every station and rank.

"Men are imperfect," many could quote throughout their lives, "And we know ourselves to be. The shame of this knowledge and the guilt of its hypocritical denial may be lessened by an honest appeal to Christ, the avowal of our difference from Him, lessening not only in the penitent, but in the frank observer, shame over that self-worship which is the essence of sin.

"We may or may not 'believe' in Christ," he wrote, "Whatever that may mean," [the phrase which earned him the unending enmity of the American Board of the (REDACTED)], "but we all long dearly for an earthly counterpart, the protector and mentor of our Dreams.

"You know and revere this man's character and qualities. You are saddened and perhaps confused by his absence and delay. How could you meet him, this perfect soul?

"You will not meet him here."

Here, it was recorded, and all who heard remembered, he paused.

"Strive to become him."

The inscription of this phrase upon Halliwell's tombstone unleashed criticism, upon its unveiling, in the Press, and since, in his various biographers, and in those detractors (two of their works well-known to these readers, and needing no further identification, nor comment save to suggest they will awaken in our School's admirers appropriate reactions which, again, I need not name).

So much rancor was raised by the simple inscription, "Strive to become him," unobjectionable save for the use of the minuscule at the head of the final word. But every Riperian, and all our friends know of the speech from which the epitaph was taken, and decry the objections of the uninformed who insist that they will not be brought and do not care, to understand, preferring outrage to correction.

Halliwell suffered calumny in life for those views his putative superiors suspected of non-orthodoxy. And the furor over the head-stone certainly was, to what extent we can not say, a revenge of the cowardly against one, debarred by death, from self-defense.

For the lowercase "h" on the stone was adduced, by the Bishops, as evidence of the Pelagian Heresy: denial of the Divinity of Christ.

Fossett, ever Halliwell's defender, responded that he was pleased to discover, in the Bishopric, those sufficiently learned as to have encountered the Pelagian Heresy.

This, of course, endeared him no further to that body. And attempts were made to have Fossett "inhibited, suspended, or deposed."

Visiting New York in 1910, he encountered his friend Bishop Weld in Peacock Alley of the Waldorf Astoria. His friend warned of danger, and Fossett replied, that, in the unfortunate event, he would "go to Rome."

Weld replied that Rome would certainly abide the Heretic less than Canterbury, to which Fossett responded that in that case he would join the Democratic Party.

~

Partisan Politics, of course, have always been discouraged at St. Ives.

Fosset always held that the boys would, of course, inherit both the principles and the prejudices of their forebears; and that, attempting to inculcate the former we must take care to exclude its yoke mate.

"To that end we embrace the Classics and may then study the newspapers not as their successors, but as a contemporary evidence of their vindication."

"There is no new thing under the sun," would begin his yearly Introduction to History, "No doctrine, inspiration, depravity, heresy, or folly."

Here he would distribute his text to the boys, and the text was, to each, a copy of that day's newspaper (*The Boston Globe*).

"Here is the Robber's Cave," he would say. "They've hidden the Wisdom of the World, in this cheap paper, it is our happy task to bring it to Light. To do so we will read it in the mirror."

He would then ask a boy, to pick, at random, "any article, any article at all." A report of political rancor would ignite a discussion of Bismark, Tsar Peter, Elizabeth, or Caesar, "playing dominoes with the world."

That of a grisly murder, Hamlet, Othello, Jael and Sisera, Pinchas, or the Code of Hammurabi.

A bold lad would suggest the sports page, prompting a discussion of David and Goliath, or the ritual sacrifices of the Mayans. Or he would quote from Tacitus on Sport, or the Norman Trial by Ordeal—"those chronicles of single combat, what do you think they were but the Sporting News? And now, read in the mirror, what is the Sporting News but the record of our chosen Knights, their victory proving the personal superiority of their adherents—we that are thus proved the elect of God?"

Inevitably, some lad would read an advertisement, and Fossett would smile and counsel, "never admit you doubt as irrational the Divinity of Christ, or that Mohammed Ascended, upon his horse, into Heaven, you who accept, unthinkingly, that an abrasive sweetened clay, rubbed on your teeth, will find you a mate. Whereby we might perceive a connection between our so-called 'modern thought,' and similar magical thinking in the Past, the extirpation of Witches; and various and ineradicable operations of the Pagan mind, still operating in a toothpaste ad.

"We, speaking as a Christian, may believe or disbelieve in the Divinity of Christ, but it is a thoughtless error to dismiss it as 'unreasonable.'

"May we rid ourselves of folly? The study of history establishes that we may not. Education exists not to inculcate wisdom, but, much more attractively, to teach the identification of folly. Let us consider it as strategy. Many of you play team sports. Do you not find it helpful, in your football game, to have studied the other side's strategy? Respond 'Yes, Sir.'

"Here we do the same. Our team is Character, let us call our opponents Human Nature.

"We can but with difficultly perceive their tactics on the field, for we are there engaged in all-out struggle.

"But they have, thoughtfully, left their playbook lying around, and we may study it at leisure. It is called the Newspaper."

And here he would assign to each an article, editorial, or advertisement.

"These are the same events, prejudices, and blandishments which have troubled man from the beginning. They have been treated by the great writers of old. Your task is to find whence these plagiarists of today have stolen their material, and explain to our team their crime."

He would then raise the shade covering the blackboard and reveal his "beloved list of fifteen books."

"Human history is the record of sex, violence, sin, treason, perversion and madness. Here" (pointing to the board), "you may find helpful guides to your investigations.

"I am sorry to expose you to the shocking, the salacious, the outlandish, and the cruel. And bid you be strong in your dedication. Spare yourselves and spare us nothing. Tell us about the World."

Fossett was asked, in his last days, how many boys, did he feel, had profited from his unorthodox approach.

"From the study of History, perhaps some," he said, "perhaps some. From my heterodoxy, I do believe, some greater number."

Our tradition of heterodoxy, of course, dates back to him, and his teaching of Greek.

His method, so successful here, was attempted and abandoned by the Seven Brothers of the New England Convention.[9]

9　The sentence continues, in the original, "as offensively effective."

Fossett had always opposed our membership in "The Communion," as he termed it, proclaiming that he saw no reason to expand a "Council of Mediocrity," past that number he could comfortably refute over one glass of bad sherry.

He held, in his defense, and not unreasonably, that his methods worked, and if their demonstrable success was insufficient to convince the merely theoretical, the inquisitive were welcome to come to his class and watch.

On his retirement the School did, in fact, join the Convention; and prior to his removal (to his brother's house, at Leamington), their Board of Governors asked him to attend the Spring Meeting, where they would announce a Special Award, to be bestowed every two years, for extraordinary achievements in education—such to be called The Jellicoe Plaque.

The invitation was replied to by his attorney, who declined "what you perhaps call an honor," adding that any use whatever of his client's name would result in legal action.

From his diary for 9 April 1921, "who would delight in the endorsement of a congeries of fools in Boston?"

He lived to see his methods, long disputed, misunderstood, and traduced, in his final years, endorsed by various panels of educators; much to his disgust—he who famously held that one or two of his boys had "perhaps learned something from a teacher, but who on earth had learned any thing from an Educator?"

His opinions on the instruction of languages were learned, as he said, in "The Best Possible School."

A resident of Tokyo (1892–1895), he learned Japanese and worked as a civilian employee of their Imperial Army as a translator (from the French) of various Military theses. At the outbreak of the First Sino-Japanese War, 1894, he was offered employment by the Japanese Army, with an equivalent rank of Lieutenant. This they considered a great and signal honor. He declined.

Having accepted employment by the Army he was, he was informed, under law, subject to conscription. He refused to serve, and spent the years 1894–1895 as a convict, "denied the Honor of a Military Prison," confined in a Prisoner of War Camp outside Kyoto.

In the Camp, "in order to survive, and, more importantly, to hear the stories," he learned several dialects of Chinese, "and enough Korean to order a sandwich."

His quip, "If a three-year-old child can learn German, why cannot I do the same?" was, later made famous (in, he graciously held, "a coincidental spontaneously created insight"), by a famous language school. Fossett denied any credit, holding that the observation was obvious.

So in the two years of his war, he became fluent not only in the two Asian languages as above, but in the Russian of his fellow prisoners; and was honored by his fellow prisoners for teaching them the languages of the other inmates.

He brought his perceptions to us, and it was indeed a fortunate day when he presented himself here in January 1919.

He showed the head, Jellicoe, the clipping from the Northeast Educator, and announced himself ready to fill that advertised spot (Teacher of Languages). Asked for his vitae he had none. University degrees, he had none. Jellicoe said, "Why should I hire you to teach languages?" And Fossett said, "Because I can." Jellicoe asked, "How might I know?"

The boys were just returning from the Winter Term and were playing in the snow in front of the Hall.

Fossett said, "Pick a boy at random. Or better, choose one whose ability you doubt. Let me sit with him till Supper, after which you will find us conversing in Russian or Japanese, your choice."

Jellicoe endorsed the trial, and was "delighted but not surprised" at supper, to witness Fossett's success; for there was, in his words, "that calm assurance about the man which inspires confidence. And it was not charisma, for there was nothing particularly noteworthy about his demeanor or appearance. His simple speech was the product not of any lack, but of a reserve bespeaking complete confidence and honesty."

Fossett taught himself Latin and Greek, and he taught them to the boys, employing the same lessons he had learned which a prisoner: "the speaker is trying to communicate *something*. If your life, your freedom, or your comfort depended upon it, you would figure out what that is. You can do likewise now." And so they did.

It was his practice to take the new boys, on the first day of Term, for Greek. He preferred to begin with Greek, to establish as myth that it was the more difficult of the two classical tongues. Challenged that it was "written in a foreign alphabet," he would reply, "It is a *code*. Where is the boy who can resist a code?"

But, he insisted, and the Heads complied, that the boys come to his Fourth Form, Introduction to Greek, hungry. They had one cup of tea for breakfast and were given no lunch.

They came to his class after the noon hour and saw, on his desk, a platter of hot scones, and one of toast; jars of jam and honey, and a stack of plates. He bid them welcome in Greek and motioned them to take their seats which they did.

He then asked, in Greek, "Are you hungry?" He would bid one boy stand, and ask, again, "Are you hungry?" In Greek, motion to the food and say, "This is food. Are you hungry?"

They were, indeed, hungry. And confused. But he insisted, as would a Greek captor of a Scythian slave, that any who wished to eat must say so in Greek. Grammar, was, on the first day, indeed, throughout the first term, unimportant, as it would be to the captor and the slave. The task of the two (and what else, traditionally is the teacher-student relationship, as he would say) is to communicate, not at some future time, but in the first instant.

He would pick up a scone, and hold it toward the boy, asking in Greek, "Are you hungry? Yes?" (A happy expression), or "No" (its opposite). The boy would respond, in Greek, "Yes." And Jellicoe would smile, and, half-offering the treat say, "this is food. *Food.*" He would motion the boy to respond "Food."

Fossett would ask, "Do you *want* food?" The boy would nod, and Jellicoe would motion, "*Say* it." Prompted with Io for I, the boy would say "want food," and had just uttered his first sentence in classical Greek. Jellicoe would pass him the scone, and call each boy up, and interrogate him similarly. Each boy would admit to wanting food and would be rewarded with a scone.

Fossett would write, in Greek, on the blackboard, Hunger, Food, Want, I, You. Pronouncing each word as he did so.

The boys were invited to return as often as they wished to the table and, there, were questioned about the words on the board. Jellicoe would point to one, and the boy would respond in Greek.

∾

Fossett was a great admirer of Marshal Saxe, "The tutor of Napoleon."

He often quoted, "attack the strong point, and the rest must fall." This proved most effective in delaying the study of Latin until the attainment of Greek (reversing the traditional progression). The transition to French ("which is basically English"), then approached as a mere elaboration of an existing skill.

He held court in the Common Room after the First War, where he, with the endorsement of the Head (then Chambers) had covered the Long Wall with a map of the world, colored to show the shifting balances of power in the restructuring of Europe. His display and his commentaries were prized not only for his mastery of European Languages (he spoke eight or nine), but for his theoretical and practical understanding of political strategy as a preliminary to warfare. Many an Old Boy, now an Officer, returned to school for Founder's

Day, to retrieve a son for the holidays, or with no excuse whatever, to avail himself of Fossett's wisdom.

During World War II, Fossett was offered a Post (and a high Military Rank), in the Office of Strategic Services (an offer which would be repeated, though he was then approaching seventy, on that organization's transformation into the CIA). Both offers he refused, confessing himself, however, always available, at School, to saddle alumni, the Armed Services, or his Country with his conjectures.

Major General Albert Conn (St. Ives, 1929) wrote of that "something more than conjecture":

> Czechoslovakia had fallen. I'd returned from liaising with the British Government, and was awaiting reassignment from the War Office to a Combat Unit, for it was obvious that we'd be in it soon.
>
> I'd spent the Battle of Britain summer in London, and by no means shared Churchill's conviction that the Germans would not now invade.
>
> The Boston house was empty, my wife had taken the children out West, and I was not due in Washington until the Monday, one long weekend away.
>
> Those of my friends who were already in the Service were dispersed to their various posts, or, if on leave, to their summer retreats. I was in that well-known state of limbo where solitude and company are equally intolerable.
>
> I decided on an act of Charity. I would drive to St. Ives, to pay my respects to Fossett. I would there give myself the gift not only of filial piety, but of his knowledge of the War I knew he was following so closely in the press.
>
> I was unconscionably pleased with my charitable behavior, never realizing till so many years later that my trip was that of a

small boy frightened and afraid to admit hurt, seeking the comfort of his father. How pompous he must have thought me, with my fatuous Soldier manner, he who had seen so much of war.

I drank his scotch, the afternoon wore on, and he found me talked-out, staring sadly at the Long Wall, and his map.

"What are you looking at?" He said.

"Sir," I said, "I am looking at the English Channel."

"No, there will be no invasion, Albert," he said, "there will be no invasion."

"How can you know, Sir?" I said.

"Because," he said, as if explaining a quality of physics, "the Devil cannot cross Salt Water."

I saw that this was not a witticism, to him, but an expression of fact.

I do not know to what intuitions Fossett had access, but I do know this one hint suggested their extensiveness and depth.

I do not know whether to call it Pagan, or Christianity *"avant la Lettre,"* I know only that in 1940 he intuited the progress of that dreadful war, and that his certainty of its outcome cheered and encouraged me, and, thus, perhaps those who served under me.

(From *A European War, Italy and France,*
Major General Albert Conn, 1949)

AUDACITY AND INSPIRATION

Fossett put his knowledge of Japanese to use in the Service of his Country after Pearl Harbor.

In retirement, and unwell, he, when summoned by one of his "Old Boys," responded, as per usual, "like the Old Firehorse."

Anson Merrill, St. Ives, '23, West Point, '28, was, then a Major in Army Intelligence. He had been given the task of creating *ab initio*, a program for instruction in the Japanese Language.

Our American Speakers, Ishei and Nisei, were being imprisoned, and the number of Caucasians fluent in the language was few. Merrill had dragged the Personnel files and discovered one Hiram Bagwell, who listed "fluent in Japanese" on his Army Induction form.

Bagwell was brought to Falls Church, Virginia, given fifty volunteers, and instructed to teach them the rudiments of Japanese. The program progressed through several months, when Merrill was asked to evaluate it.

The only speaker of Japanese he knew was his old Teacher, so he requested Fossett's help, and was not disappointed.

Fossett came down, and sat in the back of Bagwell's class in "Fifteen Basic Forms of the Japanese Verb."

Over lunch Merrill asked what Fossett thought of the class, and the Head replied he had never spent a more enjoyable morning— that Bagwell's fluency was preternatural, the worth of the instruction marred only by the fact that he was speaking gibberish.

"I could have listened forever," Fossett said. "I loved that man."

After the War Bagwell achieved a modest fame on publication of his book about the fraud, *Don't Trust Anybody*.

I know that Fossett, had he lived to see it, would have embraced the book as yet another example of his favorite proverb, "*Tourjour l'audace.*" On which subject, I am reminded of Fossett's miraculous "cure" of a very troubled youth.

This, usually happy, boy had, for some months, been exhibiting symptoms of anxiety and depression. The symptoms worsened, tardiness and inattention maturing into loss of appetite, sleeplessness, and, finally, self-inflicted wounds.

Fossett invited the boy to tea and asked how he could help. The boy denied having any problem, and all of Fossett's charm and guile were to no avail.

The meeting was occasioned by the boy's progress from knuckles left bleeding from punching a wall, to the first "hesitation marks" of an advertised attempt at suicide.

The boy's parents were out of the Country, and Fossett never had any faith in Psychiatry; the responsibility was his and he confessed himself at a loss.

"Then," he wrote, "I announced to the boy—hardly conscious that I was doing so—that I had drugged his tea—adulterating it with a hypnogogic drug which—here I looked at my watch—should be taking effect just about now.

"This was the same drug which had been administered to me by the Japanese, and I could testify that not even the strongest man could withstand its effects: that no recipient would be able to withhold a true answer to a direct question.

"I apologized for my recourse to the drug, but felt its use to by my duty, adding that the boy would, by this time, be feeling its effects—a light-headedness, and increased heartbeat—sure signs that the drug was now operating. The boy nodded that he, indeed felt the signs.

"I adopted my most Hieratic Tone and said, 'What is the Secret?' The boy replied that he had had, in his possession, since his return from the Christmas Holidays, an overdue book from the Wellesley Public Library; that the penalties, mounting month-by-month, had, even from the first, been beyond his ability to pay, and that the library's latest demand threatened legal action."

Fossett now told the boy to drink "the antidote" (a glass of water), after which he would return to normal consciousness, cleansed both of his guilt, and the memory of his experience under the drug.

When the boy had been restored to his normal state Fossett said, "It seems you have an overdue Library Book. There is no shame in this, and the solution is a simple one. We, here, in fact, have a fund available to all students earmarked just for this purpose. Give the book to me, I shall return it, and I would not be surprised if the Library, here, as in the majority of these cases, did not waive the overdue charge in gratitude for the return of the volume."

"The overdue charge was one dollar eighty-two cents," Fossett told me. "The book was *The Moving Picture Boys in Earthquake Land*, the child was driven to suicide. And we think we know something about Youth."

A PAPERWEIGHT

The paperweight, on the desk before me, reminds me of a sort of Religious conversion.

The paperweight belonged to Reginald Moore, and the conversion was mine.

It is a Vienna bronze figure of a seated spaniel. These, hand-painted, finely cast figurines were popular in mid- to late-Victorian England. Small, easily transportable, and relatively inexpensive, the beautifully wrought items served not only as mementoes of this or that Continental journey, but as bread-and-butter gifts especially acceptable as allowing the donor to exhibit thoughtfulness in the choice of objects, testifying to a recognition of the recipient's hobbies, achievements, or tastes; in horses, dogs, various generally outdoor amusements of the well-to-do; or in sly humorousness allusion to nicknames, exploits, or occurrences in a career.

Moore had somewhere acquired the old and lovingly worn seated spaniel—its look that of alert patience recognizable and moving to anyone enamored of that breed.

The paperweight might, as accurately, be named a matchsafe, for such it was. The spaniel's head hinged back to reveal the cavity which could hold a few of those old sulphureous stick matches so-favored by the boys learning (surreptitiously) to smoke, and bravely enjoying, also, thus, the odor of Hell.

One of the many contributions of Town to Gown was the shopboy's habit of igniting the sulphur match with a thumbnail, on the front teeth (really), or on the seat of the pants.

Many of the Sixth-Form boys (and no few of their younger colleagues) had endeavored to hide that scorch or burn on their trousers' bottom acquired in practice of that attractive method of ignition. Moore, as is well-known from the portraits—that in Hall, and that in the Small Room of the Library—was seldom without his pipe. It was filled and refilled with such regularity that it often outpaced the replenishment of the paperweight match-holder (such replenishment the jealously guarded prerogative of Miss Brough).

Shaking the object to discover it, as it most often was, empty, Moore would migrate to the mantelpiece, upon which rested that long, rectangular *"Mauchlinewear"*[10] box of "fireplace matches," of which he had an unending supply, they being regularly sent in bulk from James J. Fox, of London, along with a very generous (and just sufficient) monthly consignment of his Special Blend. (It was Miss Brough's duty, on several occasions, to politely decline the Tobacconist's polite request to advertise "Moore's Mixture.")

The recipe never changed, nor did he abandon the ancient red morocco tobacco pouch he had carried since his youth—in spite of the numerous gifts of pouches, boxes and humidors—many expensive and ornate—and one, in particular, a priceless antique (this last the gift of an Old Boy, just debarred, by a Turn of Fate, from accession to a very exalted Title).

These accoutrements, and the accompanying lighters, tampers, smoking tools (the pipes were treated separately), and tobaccoiana of every description, were packed and housed in The Lumber Room, and, on the Tenth Anniversary of Moore's death, auctioned at a meeting of the New York St. Ives Club—all proceeds going to the Scholarship Fund. (The amount may be found in *The Serial*, of August of that year. The School has been and remains enabled to aid

---

10 Victorian papier-mâché and wooden souvenir items made in Scotland. Ed.

many boys, due to the proceeds in that auction, and its management in the General Fund by that Financial House whose owners have served the school through, now, the fourth generation.)

The accoutrements were auctioned and sold—sale of the one most lavish item with the stipulation that identity of neither the bidder nor the amount would ever be revealed.

The purchased item was donated to the Metropolitan Museum of Art, where it may be found, still today, as part of the Arabian Craftsmanship exhibit, the accompanying plaque identifying it as a "gift of Mr. Moore."

The foot-long fireplace matches retained their place on the mantel. Miss Brough, or her various tweenies[11] (in the early days, before the local young women went, if unmarried, into the factory; and, later, into the wider world), would use the unwieldy things to light the morning fire into which they would discard the long match. This was a sight which always irritated Moore, which irritation, Mrs. Houk (née Barbara Moore) wrote, was, her father had told her, the inspiration for his commencement speech (1922) on "The Irrational."

"For who can tell from whence comes our unreasoned prejudice? The Tommies of the B.E.F. held, generally, no hatred for their German cousins, just across No Man's Land; the fury of combat and the loss of friends inspires, of course, a violent desire for both victory and revenge, but the cessation of hostilities in 1918 restored, in the hearts of the British soldier (him of the working class) the status *quo ante* of solidarity with the *deutsche arbeiter* who, but lately, he had lived to kill.

"The war was 'put to one side,' and its various hatreds, employed by Briton and German alike, now transferred to industrialists, capitalists, profiteers, and, in short, any who, though fit to serve,

---

11 Tweenie: a young maid-of-all-work. (Obsolete) Ed.

contrived to be excused—many sheep herded with the goats. So much for 1919."

~

The propaganda slogans of German barbarity proved to be largely invention, and the national hatreds they inspired, having outlived their purpose, where not only forgotten at the war's end, but, if recalled, disbelieved.

The subsequent barbarities of the next act of that thirty years war were, in contrast, though amply demonstrated, disbelieved at the time, and, after the War, debunked; sufficiently inhuman, barbaric and universal to stun the faculty of belief, the faculty itself was suspended, and the resultant neurosis of its suspension led to anger, not against the savagery, but against its victims. And Peace was made once again with Germany, its behavior being consigned to that most useful or "third" category of phenomena, that which both did and did not take place.

In his final commencement speech Moore alludes to the sharp word he had uttered to the new parlor maid discovered lighting the fire with the wrong matches. "I cherished not only my—as I thought—rational anger, but, on reflection, the laudable humility of my apology. I did not, however, thereafter cherish the shame I felt for both of the above.

"The face of the murderer is red, as is that of the victim of humiliation. And what can expunge the wrong done to those subject to my wishes, deprived of recourse, and in fact constrained to accept the apologies of one just incontrovertibly proved to think himself their superior?"

~

Moore taught his several House-Heads, and they taught theirs, the danger of idiosyncrasy.

"That which may be enjoyed or tolerated in a superior would be understood as clownish imposition in an equal, and, discovered in an employee, be understood as a demand to be discharged, such request happily granted instanter.

"How can an offender make his peace with his victim?

"What of contrition, confession, resolve, and, for those fortunate enough to be of that Communion, Absolution?"

Moore's peroration (in the ms.) began with a reference to Sherrock, who had been for many years the School's Head Gardner. He'd refused the title Groundskeeper, on two occasions, the first, a suggestion of the Head (Jellicoe), the second an offering of a well-meaning member of the Alumni Building Committee, who had had fashioned and affixed to Sherrock's office door, a bronze plaque engraved "with the more lofty title."

Sherrock unscrewed the plaque, puttied the holes, and painted, quite expertly, to match the woodgrain of the old oak door. He mailed the plaque and screws to the home of the offending Committee Member, addressing him by his "New Boy" cognomen, in place of the man's subsequent titles and honors, added to the superscription in both parentheses and quotation marks. "If there is shame in being a gardener," he had written, "I have yet to discover it. Should I do so, I believe myself honest enough to mend my ways without your prompting. If you believe your fellow Christian incapable of that, I suggest you soil yourself with no further intercourse with such a man." Moore related (ms.) how the letter's recipient, ex-Lieutenant Governor of his state, and Chairman of the Board not only of his family's corporation, but of the United Philanthropies of New England, on receipt of the letter and the plaque, drove, through one hundred miles of January snows, to St. Ives, to the Gatehouse, where he begged, in a boy's tears, to be forgiven for his presumption.

Which, boy, of course, he was.

We find, in the margin of Moore's ms., the note, "God bless the Scots."

For it was Sherrock to whom the Old Boys referred most often. In their letters to the School, to the Heads, to home, in battlefields from three wars, and to the boy's favorite of his maxims: "Life is a journey; and as with any journey, we usually find we've packed the wrong things."

Moore, it was said, had once used the fireplace matches to make a splint for a bird's broken leg.

This was a pure invention of the type accruing to any beloved character living at one remove.

The Old Boys would, on any occasion, send him a pipe (we have noted his collection), and these he would display in the glass-fronted case he'd received, on his 30th Anniversary, from the Association.

But he only smoked his old Canadian, much loved, much repaired. The gift pipes—beautiful burled wood, exotic meerschaums, amber or ivory stemmed—were prized but were not used. He willed these to the Association to be distributed, on his death, to its Members with a request that they include me in the distribution.

And one morning, in a year I will not name, I filled that pipe, and was taking a match from the match holder, thinking, of my happy comfort, and how lucky I was to've risen, by that well-known admixture of effort and luck to my position of honor and ease. And, for some reason, I came to doubt myself—loathing, in fact, the hypocrisy of my formulation. For some one of the successful may, in the Millennium, actually credit Luck to the detriment of Worth—who am I to say—but I was not one of these. I was a hypocrite and a fool, who had inherited a few precepts and found them practicable and pleasant to speak, and had repeated them until the process of attrition opened before me the position vacated by their original preceptors.

The magnificent attractions of Rome had long been evident to me. But here, I thought, here was the New Thing—a Religious Intimation whose overwhelming power I could but compare to nausea.

Was I being challenged to become an Anchorite? A Monk? Or, more, much more to my horror, was it not equally likely that my comfortable Episcopalian soul was tearing itself apart to allow reformation as a Dissenter, Leveler, or Puritan?

Was this not—what else could it be—that great fire which had purified the Burned-Over District, in the Second Great Awakening?[12]

The adolescent trauma of "Religious Awakening" was as familiar to me as to any who've spent their lives teaching boys. Was I experiencing a late-onset of that fervor—long understood as a concomitant of burgeoning sexuality—now, at its close?

To whom could I take my doubts, those doubts mixed with both shame and fear? The fear I discounted as mere cowardice, facing what I understood as a necessary renunciation of not only my position, and, thus, income, but of all society, which, it seemed to me, must expel from its midst a low "dissenter."

Fear to one side, I elected to analyze my feelings of shame.

Did I lack even the courage to confront my thoughts?

Were there not actual martyrs? And if Jan Hus and Wycliffe could go to the stake, perhaps one so poor as I could discover some resolve.

I was not threatened with the stake. I was, in fact, not actually threatened at all—or only by a "passing thought."

12 Religious revival of the early nineteenth century—born and centered in western New York State, known because of its intensity, consequently, as "the Burned-Over District." Ed.

But this thought had unnerved me sufficiently to drive me to fantasy of martyrdom—which must be, then, a fantasy compensatory of low self-worth. And so, my interrogatives returned me to shame.

But God had put me here, I formerly believed, and if now, my self-loathing had tempted me to doubt it, I could reason no further without accepting, if not the existence of a Creator, at least that of my placement.

Seneca taught that gods either do or do not exist. If they do, things are, thus, unfolding according to some plan. (How else to understand the operative nature of gods?) But perhaps they do not; then, why be reluctant to depart from a world without gods?

But I found that, in truth, I had never doubted the existence of God, and, thus, must allow the existence of a plan. My shame, then, I reasoned, was grown either from dereliction to or ignorance of my responsibilities.

I not only thought, but *knew* myself to be considerate, honest, and in possession of various allied and consequent gentlemanly virtues.

But, as I held, yet, the unstruck match in my hand, I realized that, as Sherrock taught, I had, on my journey, packed the wrong things— that I required not Tolerance, Good Humor, and Intelligence (all of which I possessed by nature, at no cost, and, therefore of some use but of no particular merit) but, at this stage of my life, something quite different. I had acquired doubt.

I returned to Moore's journals—those preliminary notes for sermons—and found there, as I remembered, "On Setting Off."

He here recalls his brief sojourn in Russia, part of the Grand Tour, and the Russian habit, when all is prepared and packed, and the conveyance—in this case a carriage—waits outside, of turning back from the door, and sitting, for a while.

The door, in my case, is Death, which, of course, awaits us all, but the imminence of which is plainer to those in whom the passions, mercifully, have cooled.

The views of my later life and career stem from my visitation (I will call it that) on that September morning.

Their name and nature are personal and idiosyncratic. Some may care to deduce them from my behavior. If such can be done, please allow me to confess myself content.

The sermon which came to my mind, contemplating the match-safe, was Moore's, "The Four Who Did Not Jump." This was his biblical commentary, reprinted, in *The Serial* of June 1946, but given, in his Datebook as of the previous May, as supported by the reminiscences of the attendees.

The date is significant, if (as is above supposed) it was the eighth of May (a Sunday), which would have been the one-year anniversary of VE Day. The sermon dealt with cowardice.

Thirteen thousand American paratroopers enplaned to jump into Nazi-held Europe on D-Day. Four refused to jump. His sermon is, if not well-known, easily accessible, having been privately printed several times, and distributed, not only at School, but at Alumni functions, and those of Veterans Groups, both as religious and even corporate-promotional literature.

Moore's notebooks, originally in possession of his grand-niece, and, now a part of the American Education Archive of Dartmouth College give the full text of the sermon as typed. But many attendees recall a section which does not appear there; and, so, if they are to be credited, must have been delivered *ex tempore*. The most-often recalled component of which was Psalms 38:18, "For I am prone to Gripping Pain, and my Ache is always before me. Because I admit my iniquity."

The Memorialists all mention the "over long" or "extended" pause which proceeded the improvisation, a look of pain on his face as he peered through the chancel window of The Red House.

Was this, they wondered, a reference to our recurrence of sorrow regarding the recent school tragedy—the suicide of Mrs. Williams—and, if so, what was the cowardice to which the Head alluded? Was it that affair from reference to which he was debarred by his sense of propriety, his heart perhaps heavy with knowledge of which he could neither unburden himself, nor disclose with equanimity?

Which of us has been fortunate enough to have avoided a similar situation?

This, it was reported, was the end of his digression *mori quam foedari* ("death before dishonor"), retained in my most recent correspondent's memory these many years, ". . . after most other precepts have been winnowed away. This remains as most easily retained, as a statement of morality primarily, and more importantly, as a mechanical principle of operation—as, in any case whatever, the more cost-effective choice."

Mrs. Williams is remembered today as the (do they consider her fictional?) heroine of the (avowable version of) the Drinking Song of TOP.[13]

---

13 Note: She was, in her day, though a staunch Democrat, Feminist, and Egalitarian, a supporter "in its trial" of TOP—its existence called into question by the ad hoc "Committee of Investigation," newly-promoted Graduates taken with the "Armchair Bolshevism" of the 1930s. I addend its defense published in *The Misfit* (Summer 1935), under the name Edmund Burke, but long supposed to have been written by her or at her direction:

"The Secret Society for the freedom of which all men long is called Maturity. It is discovered, by the fortunate, in the most necessarily restrictive of societies: marriage and the family, the Army and the Church. In these the individual may enjoy solidarity and other legitimate delights; there, however, the intimate constriction of Membership and its responsibilities preclude the adolescent cant of 'Liberty.'

"Boundless Liberty cannot be other than savagery.

"A constriction, mutually agreed to between Member and Authority, supplies that path upon which, and only upon which, the individual may be free to progress in *individuality*.

Mr. Lane Griffiths (St. Ives, 1930-1960) was the unofficial ruler of our unofficial Drama Department, and the self-described "Avatar of Comus." As such he organized and staged those Classics enjoyed every year (and still) in Spring Term.[14]

He was always to be found, wrapped in his scarf, in the third row at rehearsals, and muttering, ". . . each man kills the thing he loves." It is reported that after the suicide of Mrs. Williams he used the phrase in the presence of Moore, and seeing the look on the latter's face, never uttered it again.

"Our Secret Society contains, it is true, only the chosen. But so, we may reflect, does marriage, wherein the partners choose each other.

"Does it confer privileges? (What association other than slavery does not?) What can carping be but envy?

"Does it demand service? Look at its charter requiring charity, Mutual Aid, and Military Service."

The writer closed with a quote from Seneca. "You are denied admittance to an Entertainment? You were not meant to attend."

14　These productions quite determinedly separate from the Revels, which were always the provenance of TOP.

SELF CONFIDENCE

As a young teacher I was pressed into service as "utility man," or, more plainly, "dogsbody"—sent to serve where the illness or other absence of the assigned instructor required a "warm form" to stand in the front of the class.

Given one night's notice, I, as every teacher down through time, could prepare for the next day's assignment. One, after all, did not need to know much (one might more honestly say "any") physics, calculus, German, Natural History, and so on, in order to pass out papers, copy a diagram onto the board, or require a boy to recite. Testing was always a fig-leaf to my ignorance, and so the illusion of professorial knowledge (not to say omniscience) was, to my mind, preserved. But it was not so-preserved in the minds of those I felt myself to be deluding. I relate my unmasking.

New England rustics know "a warm winter makes a full graveyard."

Great and prolonged cold kills germs, and, more importantly, restricts (in the old Farm Days, barred) visiting.

1924-25 was a "brown winter." For the first in many years there was little snow, travel and visiting were unimpaired, and a (much milder) occurrence of the 1918 influenza afflicted many.

I was just in my first year as an instructor, and tasked with filling in for many, each of whose specific educational accomplishments easily surpassed mine, as I had none.

Thinking myself their discoverer, I employed the various dodges mentioned above. Then, like many another victim of that self-importance nurtured by (supposed) immunity, I began to believe myself possessed of the Secret of Education (I could not then, or now, name it succinctly, but it seems to be, "stand in front of the class and let the ignorant admire you").

I was brought to earth one morning because I had actually become interested in the subject I was "getting up" for the morrow.

I'd been told off to take the Sixth Form boys in Physiology.

I had some knowledge of English Literature, that discipline (or diversion) I had ostensibly been hired to teach, and some memory of mathematics and geometry—enough to get through one hour's lesson.

Of Physiology I knew only that it was a word.

The instructor (may his Shade forgive me, I have forgotten his name, and I owe him much), had left no lesson plan, save a note card, on which was scrawled the lesson's date. The note was used as a bookmark, the book held pride of place, dead center on his desk, and I guessed that the chapter marked indicated the subject of the next day's lesson.

I began to read. And as I read, I made the mistake of becoming interested.

The chapter dealt with peas, and the work of Genetics, that science, I learned, founded by Gregor Mendel, upon his study of the things.

Well, yes, I also learned a black dog and a white dog, mated, will produce, in one litter, one black dog, one white dog, and two parti-colored dogs, or some such.

Yes, I became interested, and, there came to the fore that defect which has plagued me through life, I began to overelaborate an unschooled first impression into a general theory, not only of the subject involved, but, as Pet once said, "of all life on Earth."

It occurred to me, dreaming over the book, that Mendel's "theory of Dominance" could be observed among the boys at school (who were, after all, my particular Pea Garden).

They, it seemed, brought forth the dominant and suppressed the recessive traits in that conjunction, not of genes, but of *dispositions*, congealing as the group, in the House, or the Team.

Yes, in the admixture of personalities, the dominant boy would encourage supporters, the recessive boy protectors—groups inferior (in need or skill) to these poles would accrete as imitators or adherents, each group now containing an admixture of the two polar qualities.

I fell asleep cogitating, or, say, dreaming over my book.

The Physiology class was, of course, the first of the day. The boys were prepared to spend the hour in study, having been so-advised by the Head, on learning of the illness of—it occurs to me now, it was Horace Winsted.

But I was full of myself, of my new toy, genetics, and my cherished all-purpose tool, the ability to "change the level of abstraction."

(Pet once said that, as a child, returning home with a skinned knee, I, rather than fetching her a cold compress, began to lecture her on the genius of the ball-and-socket joint.)[15]

And so, I shared my enthusiasm for my fresh-chosen field of Genetics with the Sixth-Form boys, who, as they had been studying it for half a year, were as Solons to my untutored presumption. The hour struck, class was dismissed, and I thought myself well-acquitted.

---

15 She told the story at one of my birthday parties. I laughed with the rest, but suggested that the knee was *not* a ball-and-socket joint. She replied that she knew that at the time, but preferred to suffer the pain of a skinned knee rather than witness that of my shame should she correct me.

"Why," I thought (as any who remember their first days might admit), "there is nothing *to* this teaching!"

Mr. Winsted returned to his class, and I to my regular duties, with that magnificent self-confidence increased by triumph-over-odds.

Which feeling persisted until the appearance, in the Spring number of *The Misfit* of a cartoon.

The cartoon showed me "treating" a group of six boys at the Tuck Shop. The waitress is bearing a platter full of covered dishes. I am lecturing: "Now boys, we have ordered bacon and eggs. You will see that, distributed among you, randomly, will be one plate of bacon, one of eggs, two of Pikkens, and two of Chigs." [16]

---

16 *The Misfit* ceased production during WWII. This issue along with the rest was lost in the fire of 1961. The jest survives in the names of the Fourth-Form's intramural teams.

PEDAGOGY EXAMINED

> ". . . and early theories, ruined by observation,
> and, through practice, refined into newer theories,
> which, in turn themselves, et cetera . . ."
> from *Moore's Journal*

What finally was left of it—it being a School—save the teacher, the student, and the board of Epictetus on which they sat? The essential question, then, shorn of bureaucracy, and Place and Position, "What did I, and, thus, the School, have to teach?"

For, in absolute truth, what is there, of languages classical or modern, of mathematics, or the music from which it derives, of even the various sub-species and needless proliferations of disciplines that cannot be learned more easily from a book?

Is it not a cherished myth (no less true for that) that this or that statesman writer or jurist never attended one day's schooling? More importantly, do we not, one and all, attribute the individuality and concision of his thought to the lack?

Then what of school and what of our professions, true or factitious, but in any case unexamined, of its worth?

Filial piety, of course, is not to be despised, but it may be understood, for all it is hailed (and may in fact be) a virtue, as a mere physiological response.

As such it is one with the love of parents and infants, the first perceiving in their progeny imaginary—or at least not yet revealed—talents and quaint habitudes, the second, bred, by the need to survive, to display a helplessness sufficiently charming as to dissuade its masters from dispatching them as the most efficacious response to their demanding uselessness.

Thus nature and custom fashion a system of mutual education, subsuming two parties of widely differing needs, through a genetically inspired necessity evolving into Culture. In one case, the Family, in another, later abstraction, the School.

The link between teacher and student, however, is not genetically inspired, and, thus, rests upon no *a priori* mutuality.

Pedagogy attracts, *inter alia*, the martinet, the paedophile, the time-server, the petty bureaucrat, the pompous. (The reader may expand the list according to his own experience. I doubt he will be moved to reduce it.)

The love of youth, and the love of teaching, may conceal even from their professors, motives and propensities best kept in check.

We note, we must note, also the myth of Pygmalion and Galatea—for who does not fall in love with his own creations?

This affection, name it what one will, can be found in even the most chaste of teachers, and in the reciprocal affection of the created; and must be accounted, on both sides (to what degree in each, to be determined by the individuals), a component of that affectionate society of the Alma Mater.

How to maintain the necessary divide between young and old, between Eros and Philos, and, the more mundane distinction between buyer and seller?

For students are, effectively, consumers of that service contracted for by their elders. And teachers are purveyors of that contracted service. How very often this mercantile reality has been ignored—not overlooked, but consigned to the psychological netherworld of the disagreeable, ill-bred, and, finally, the inconvenient.

But any honest investigation must begin with the most basic of facts—and there is no better clue to their irreducibility than a feeling of aversion.

Someone pays.

We may, from this, proceed to the question: for what?

If this question cannot be answered in words as few short and concise as would the same question asked of a mechanic, the question must be posed again, until it either is blessed with a reply of equal simplicity, acknowledged to be unanswerable, or of that class to which an answer would be inconvenient.

"Freedom of Thought," "Intellectual Curiosity," and similar supposed end-products are as happily abstract as was "Gentility" to the public schools of England.

For if possession or attainment of the end product is not contracted for and specified, how will the notional purchaser know it has been supplied?

He will not. Which is the beauty, to the school, of the formulation. (See also, the unstated, as unstateable, assertion of the Psychoanalyst, that, after a course of treatment the purchaser might "be," or "feel" "better.")

The rational ("boorish" or "underbred") consumer, unwilling to engage in the above charades, might likely say "I will not buy it"; as, "I already have all of the 'nothing' I require."

One pays the butcher for a leg of lamb. It is forthcoming or not. If not, the purchase price may be withheld. If supplied, its quality and weight may be debated. But how is one to evaluate a transaction which has no discernable product?

The question itself has been marginalized as déclassé; acceptance of which formulation has enabled the great universities and their imitators, one generation after another, to merchandise that which "dare not say its name."

Its name is Status, which may further be reduced to the delusion that the waste of money will somehow raise one in the estimation of some unspecifiable group.

What might this group be? And could one rationally suppose such convened especially for the purpose of evaluating one's purchases? Yes, perhaps. But even if so, who would, on reflection, strive to seek the approval of such a group?

One might respond, "But is there not such a thing as 'group approval,' and the security deriving there from?"

Of course there is. And that security may be understood as the (real or not, but certainly not limitless) protection of group membership; and, the security of freedom from thought deriving therefrom.

Such exists, as all but the Stylite are aware. And, perhaps, that is the ultimate reduction of our search.

Perhaps the school exists to sell that security called "fashion." Well and good, and who is immune?

Someone wrote there is no satisfaction, even that of perfect religion understanding, surpassing the knowledge that one is perfectly dressed.[17] *Disons le mot*: elite schools exist to sell fashion, as does *haute couture*. This, of course, may supply the covering of nakedness and protection from cold found in the most utilitarian of garments; and, we, speaking of the School, may, equally, and so on . . . (To torture the conceit.)

The schools sell fashion, and, so, merchandise the hypothetical (for who can finally say in what fashion exists, or what momentary and instant whim of the mob may render that of yesterday loathsome and reveal today's certainty as foolish on the morrow?). Education then (the actual demonstrable accession, in the student of skill not previously possessed), must be considered (when not an actual hindrance in the prime task) a happy byproduct.

---

17   Ed. Note: It was Shaw.

Now we may, without shame, and, indeed, with perhaps some pride, overcome and recognize the folly of the suppositional exchange, and reduce (if not hypocrisy, then the absurdity) of such to reason.

Here is the test of a true education, the application of which, alone, can preserve its practitioner and consumers in dignity:

What exactly is being promised?

Does the consumer assent to such instruction?

What does it cost?

How may progress be evaluated?

If the student (to use an unfortunately widespread example), after three or four years of "taking" French cannot speak French, the school is a fraud, and the consumer (though a victim) a party to fraud.

The wise parent would demand specificity in the curriculum mooted for his son, and subsequent performance on the part of the school. A school failing performance should refund tuition *pro rata* with its failures.

"This simple expedient would do much—and that instantly—to reform that which passes as education" (Edward Jellicoe, 1905).[18]

---

18 Jellicoe was asked "what of the 'bad boy,'" the obtuse, resistant, or recalcitrant, who "would not be taught." He suggested that such students be rejected, much as the physician rejects those appealing for his help who may be ill. (op cit.)

THE DEATH WATCH

"We are all, of course, more acute in discerning sin in others than in ourselves.

"As we become aware of this tendency we compound our presumption, explaining that we, whose good motives we know, are thus exempt from blame; and that even those actions obviously wrong in others are, performed by us, either justifiable per se, or acceptable when taken in average with our otherwise moral behavior.

"It is difficult to admit to sin. How much more difficult to confront in ourselves its justification?

"For sin may be forgiven, and, indeed, forgotten, but who forgets the shame of admitted hypocrisy?"

These were the words of Jellicoe, published by his daughter, Mrs. Larson, as part of that collection commemorating the tenth anniversary of his death, the above, from a section titled *Apologia*.

It is unclear if the title is his or hers. I suspect the former, for it is a strong word, and, I feel, over-harsh, especially for that which might be taken (as posthumous) as a peroration. It is not. The collection must be understood (as chosen and arranged), as the vision of its *editor*.

I am put in mind of the Vaudeville Shows of my youth. They were constructed of five or seven acts: the dance, the jugglers, the magician, singer, dancer, a comedy routine, or brief play in the "olio"; each act stood alone. However, the evening, I was told by an old

Vaudeville Entertainer,[19] was structured to mimic those emotions one might experience at a drama or tragedy, and in the same order in which they might there occur. Viz: introduction, relaxation, complication, surprise, wonder, confusion, enlightenment, self-doubt, repletion, and so on. So must it be with any collection, not the least that under discussion here. For I cannot help but think that Mrs. Larson put, or allowed to be inferred, too much emphasis on Jellicoe's regrets.

The recognition of failure is common to all professions practiced by the serious man. For the laity, we know, put far too much faith in our protestations, both of expertise and humility; and allow over much respect to our position.

It is the excellent man, indeed, who will not, occasionally, rely on such respect. We all grow weary, and, indeed, confused, and even despondent over the gap between our abilities and our responsibilities.

We may shelter ourselves in hypocritical diffidence—who is the man who has not tried?—and must, in honesty, find it no shelter at all.

We may also seek solace in *confession*.

But abjection is so easily warped into that false humility which, if the gods detest Hubris, is certainly detested by the gods.

Mrs. Larson knew her father as I did not. But I knew him well, and in a capacity which, similarly, was unknowable to her.

---

19   The entertainer is likely Otto Gustav Greunz, "Fritz, the Bicycle Comic." He was a headliner of the Keith-Orpheum Vaudeville circuit in the period prior to World War One, when the anti-German hysteria forced his retirement from the Stage. Hollis wrote, in his diary of 1912, "May Ten, Moore and I went down to the colonial. On the bill, Otto (my favorite). His 'turn' involves coming on, wheeling a bicycle, and leaning it against the side of the stage, and then delivering a monologue. We went back afterward, and he received us graciously, and held forth, for some time, about Show Business, closing with the 'profound wish' that we would only enjoy it from the safety of the Audience."

He was a great teacher; and, if an artist is one gifted by God with intuition, and dedicated to its perfection, he was an artist.

Where is the artist without severe doubts? He is called a hack, to whom nothing is more enjoyable than false protestations of unworthiness?

But I note the one essay, in *Apologia*, and will come to Dr. Jellicoe's defense on the charge of merchandising forgiveness for sin—this, known of old as "simony."

I believe his essay on "The Death Watch" is a joke, and intended as such.

I suggest, in support, its similarity to his sermon on Jonah. (Op cit.)

Jonah is dispatched to Nineveh, disguises himself, and takes ship for Tarshish. A great storm comes, and the sailors realize there is one on board who has offended God. Jonah says, "Yes, it is I," and is thrown overboard. The "great fish" keeps him in its belly for three days and spews him out at Nineveh. He marches around the city shouting, "Repent and be saved,'" and the citizens repent. He sits under a tree, wondering, I believe, *"Was there not a simpler way, God, to accomplish this . . . ?"*

I find the same phrase, concluding "The Death Watch." (The diary entry, of course, originally untitled, the title added by Mrs. Larson.) In form and tone, the essay mimics his early sermon on Jonah.

He is implored, by a Board member, to come to New York on "a matter of utmost urgency." He travels to New York and meets with Dr. (DELETED). He is tasked to raise money for the school.

Informed that they are "planning an assault" on (DELETED), a dying philanthropist, Jellicoe is asked to announce himself in New York on school affairs, and eager to meet the man, *whom he is not to know is dying.*

Jellicoe demurs, citing the Hippocratic Oath: has the Physician forgotten that he has sworn to reveal nothing of what passes between him and his patient?

He is told that the patient's information came to the physician "completely by accident," that it was overheard, in the conversation of two of his colleagues, while changing out of their golfing attire in the North Shore Country Club locker room.

But still, Jellicoe says, "Are you not bound . . ."

He is, unsurprisingly, upbraided for his "lack of realism."

No, the Physician says, No oath has been violated, but you, Jellicoe, have a duty to act upon information which may be beneficial to our school.

Jellicoe says he must sleep on it.

He retires to his usual room at the Yale Club.

He refuses various offers of company and eats alone.

After dinner he sits alone over his port in the reading room. Engaged in that dialogue well known to all: is he being over-nice? Is he, in fact, being destructively careful when it is his job to be bold?[20] The scales tip this way, and they tip that. He castigates himself, now, under a third head: he may do the questionable thing, or he may do the passive, but, in his inability to decide, he self-convicts of cowardice.

"Port," he wrote, "is not the beverage best-suited for this harrowing of the soul." He orders a whisky, and then another.

"I had always thought," he writes, "that it is impertinence to beg from the Almighty a service I am unwilling to perform myself. But here I asked not only for guidance, but for a 'sign,' which is to say, for that decision I was reluctant to make.

"I knew, as one does, the correct decision. It is simplicity itself to determine, as it will always be the more painful of two; nonetheless I cravenly prayed to God for a sign, which sign would relieve me of responsibility.

---

20 The School had suffered greatly in the Panic of 1893. This had erased the bulk of the Endowment, and had caused the curtailment of construction on the Annex.

"As I prayed a college classmate (Yale) sat in the chair opposite. He reached across the table for a match for his cigar and commented on the whisky decanter in front of me. 'Unusual drink for you, Edward,' he said, 'Drowning our Sorrows?' 'Something like that,' I said. 'Well, then,' he said, 'your Misery has company,' and he called for and filled a glass.

"'And what is *your* particular dilemma?' I said.

"'Mine, as many today, is financial,' he said. 'Manhattan Trust has failed and taken with it the fortunes of many of my clients.'

"Hardly daring to hope, I asked, 'Is that of (naming the philanthropist) among them?'

"'Yes,' he said. 'He is now shorn as naked as the day of his birth. Insolvent. *And* I hear he is not well.'

"I ask you," Jellicoe wrote, "And was it not clear that Fate would, at some point, require me to requite the favor?

"As, of course, she did, in the case of (DELETED)."

~

There were the two suicides. The one—not hushed, but treated civilly with that courtesy a later day might call "repression."

Tate, it is not too much to say, was "insane with the shame of his discovery." Scions of position and wealth, and, indeed, friends of the same, have often been offered the alternative of Disappearance. This, if undeserving of the modifier "honorable," may, I believe, sometimes be characterized, even at this late date, as "decent."

For what purpose is there in shaming a man? This is, to those capable of shame, a punishment not unlike execution; and, to those incapable, no punishment at all.

~

An impromptu movement had been launched, by the New York Club, proving itself, on this occasion, as on others, the opposite of "staid and stodgy."[21]

There was a private railway car laid on, which would spirit Tate, in disguise, to San Francisco, there to meet a schooner belonging to

_____.

Tate, then, in capacity of supercargo, was to sail to the Micronesian Islands, embarking at any of his choice, and in possession not only of a large sum of gold, but of a letter of credit on Amsterdam (the possessor's name left blank for Tate's creation, and insertion) to a bank charged and empowered to support him to any length of days in complete anonymity.

That the theatricality of the plan may have appealed to the Old Boys I can neither confirm nor deny.

I do know that their purpose, independent of its charm, was the preservation of life, and that they backed their word with cash, the calling-due of several serious favors, among them the acquisition— no one then or later would say how—of an irrefutable Dutch passport (the record of which was then expunged from their National Archives), and the remote but real risk of criminal indictment for "abetting a fugitive."

Yes, there was that of the Ruritanian in the endeavor—but I believe the instigators treated this more as a happy byproduct rather than an essential aspect of the case.

Several of the sons of these projectors—not surprisingly—served, later, in the OSS, its progeny, the CIA; and in the SOE, Churchill's wartime band of brigands. These postings, in the interwar years and

---

21 "I see where the supposed probity of the Old Boys of TOP stopped short of insertion, into the Bridal Suite of the Sherry, of a nanny goat, to aid the Chevening Nuptials." (Courtesy of the family of Charles Hollister, Private Correspondence, undated.)

later, came to be expected among the products of England's Public Schools, and in the Ivy League. And thus works the blessing of fantasy in many a privileged breast. [22]

I will name but its prime proponent, our President Theodore Roosevelt (although we may not claim his line as Sons of St. Ives, but of a Sister School). We note in him, however, the (now traditional) progression—that, finally, of a boy privileged (for good and ill) to remain a boy: from Hudson River Aristocracy, to ranch hand, soldier, Police Commissioner, Politician.

Is this *nostalgie de la boue*? A taste for adventure? Perpetual adolescence? They are one-half of Plato's description of the Philosopher King, schooled in the music of Athens, and the gymnastics of Sparta. We, of course, seldom see them conjoined, but may say, of the adventurer, that perhaps he does more good (or perhaps less evil) than his passive, philosophic brother in the preservation of the State—the doctrine, of course, of that Muscular Christianity promulgated, if not practiced, with some ubiquity in an earlier time.

The case of Tate's would-be-confederates is an example, again for good and ill, of the universal love of the Boy for mischief, and his adoration for such bearing any sort whatever of license.

The generation which marshaled to Tate's aid was raised on the works of Baroness Orczy, Anthony Hope, and PC Wren (Note: *The Scarlet Pimpernel*, *A Prisoner of Zenda*, *Beau Geste*). How odd that one should have to name these to the current day. But fashions, along with every other thing, change. It is a pity they are not read today, for they are fantasies of service.

∽

---

22 "The idle rich are not idle, of course, but fully occupied in the search for amusement, the search alone offering the possibility of that amusement they crave." Fossett, Private Diaries. Ed.

I recall Edson Prentiss, ex-head of The Committee, at his country estate, in old age, sitting in his bath chair in the most beautiful of autumn afternoons.

He was quite near death. He knew it and he very much appeared to be relieved. Our conversation quieted into a perfect silence, our thoughts running, as they will, upon similar lines. He said, "His passport will be made, and crowns for convoy put into his purse."[23] He looked at me and smiled, his mind, as mine, thrown back those forty? Fifty? Years to the plan to Extract the Condemned.

Was there that in it of concern for the Honor of the School? I had never thought of it, until one Head of House, long lost in the flight to Rome, suggested it to me one evening in the Common Room. I was surprised to find myself surprised. It had never occurred to me. Nor, I thought, on reflection, could it have occurred to any who knew the School of that day, and the Old Boys who, as The Brigands, had become the conspirators. Differently, if they thought (in whatever measure) primarily of the Honor of the School, I will believe they understood it, in this case, to consist in the operation of a principle: that one must not destroy a human being.

~

Boys returned to me who had been at the Liberation of the Camps, and told how they, with one impulse, slaughtered the S.S. guards and gave no more thought to it—then or after—than that with which one would kill vermin.

Life is short, and we all have to die. Those soldiers understood it as their duty to remove the monsters from life, as, equally, the Brigands of TOP understood theirs as the salvation of a life they communally and personally knew worth saving. Both actions were

---

23 St. Crispin's Day Speech, *Henry V* Act IV Sc. iii. Ed.

illegal, and performed at the risk of "their lives, their fortunes, and their Sacred Honor."

Here was the plan: an ex-Pinkerton Detective, presenting himself as still on the Force, a forged "Judge's Order to Vacate," to be presented to the head keeper of the Tremont Street jail, to secure Tate's Release. A private railway car, the service of an expert in makeup, a Dutch Passport, a ship for the South Seas, an inexhaustible line of credit and a life of anonymity were all at hand. Could G.A. Henty do more? Or Ned Buntline? (Wherein we see the actual power of Education, which is the transmission of *culture*—that the Culture here was that of fantasy devoured at leisure is the choicest clue for the education of Teachers: anyone can master a subject, your true task is to understand your *pupils*. The young boy adores fantasy as it offers him freedom. Can you do the same in teaching mathematics?)

The escape plan was put into operation.

Tate was, however, discovered in the jail by that same detective hired to shepherd him onto the Boston train, dead by his own hand, hanged by the rough noose he had fashioned from his shirt.

What was gained by his suicide? His purpose, which is to say Death. And who has, among us, not, at least, once, in the long, long night and crazed in his search for Peace, thought of Death and thanked the Lord they are the same?

He is buried, at his request, on the grounds, in an unmarked grave, whose location—it is School tradition—is revealed only to the current head of TOP, by his outgoing predecessor, who may, additionally, add or withhold his comments as he thinks good.

CHADWICK

For, as Chadwick said, there are two choices: Wisdom is either "where you find it," or "where somebody *else* finds it." In which sense it can be but mere instruction.[24] Loved and admired both as a teacher of history and as a devoted student of Scripture, he rose from Affection to Fame after his quip about a sports victory.

The school was exuberant on the Monday following our unexpected baseball triumph over St. Jude's.

Under that day's relaxed strictures of victory, one boy jocularly challenged Chadwick to find a biblical reference pertinent to our baseball triumph. He was expected to quote some triumphalist passage, and identify our institution, or our Faith, as "Israel."[25]

"It all has been written," Chadwick said, "and can be found *here*," touching the small, morocco-bound Bible always on his desk.

"Those of you interested in last afternoon's contest will have noted our chagrin, in the days preceding it, as it was not expected that we could prevail over their indomitable hitter, his name, I believe, Frost.

"You will note, also, the news transmitted by that 'bush telegraph' more swift, if not more accurate, than that of Mr. Morse, that

---

24 "The study of a map may inform us where we are, but cannot tell us either where to go or whither we may now be bound." ("Memories of Henry Chadwick," *The Serial*, #82—Summer)

25 This, of course, an ancient Episcopal tradition, holding that the Britons were one of the ten lost tribes, and converted by Joseph of Arimathea in his well-known visit to Cornwall in 55 AD.

their defeated team 'slipped bounds,' last night, and took themselves to some roadhouse to 'medicate their sorrows,' and that they have found themselves, this morning, overcome with the unfortunate sequel to overindulgence."

Here, as he had planned, one boy raised his hand, and asked Chadwick to elaborate upon his biblical exegesis of the baseball game.

"I remind you of Exodus 3-17," he said, touching his Bible, "'I shall afflict the Hittites and Heavites . . .'" Here he opened his history text.

"Now," he continued, "let us cast our minds back to that Year of Grace 1812, a year, as you know, which took its name from the great International Conflict then raging. Who can name it?"

I, who was one of his Boys, quote from memory.

~

And I recall his (slight) contretemps with a certain high Ecclesiastic, come to grace our school for a short visit in, I believe, 1912. Over the port in the Common Room this Priest commented that he had heard of this "novelty," of coupling Irony with Divine Instruction (see: the bon mot regarding St. Jude's), and, he supposed, that it could come to no great harm.

"I agree with you, Sir," Chadwick said, "save in your assertion that its use is novelty, for do we not find, in the Gospels, various instances of the same?"

Challenged to name them, he responded, "Take all you have and give it to the poor," "If someone steals your coat give him your cloak," "Struck on one cheek turn the other cheek."

The Divine assumed an expression denoting his horror of heresy, and Chadwick continued.

"Therein we find the greatest understanding of the Human Mind. For, though we all respect the teachings, and insist upon their Divinity, no man practices them in perfection. We are, thus, always struck with the difference between our professions of faith and our acts.

"Had the great Teacher merely said 'do good,' each man would rest unchallenged and content, for each thinks his acts good.

"The Lord's directives, thus, may be understood as the Cross *Implanted* in our consciousness. Through Irony, Sir; through that humor which, alone, allows us, unashamed, to confront our own hypocrisy."

He had been my history teacher, and he was the man I was fortunate enough to have as the mentor of my early teaching days.

I will add one more instance of Chadwick's thinking; he, of whom it was said, "found in everything a joke, and found all jokes worthy of study."

A stray dog had been run over and killed, on the road just inside the Gate.

There had been, for the preceding year, a sign there, reading, "Reduce speed to ten miles an hour." The sign now, proving ineffective, the Faculty went into conference.

Various ideas came to the floor and were rejected on those sundry grounds presenting themselves inevitably to any committee.

Chadwick suggested raising the speed limit.

Asked how in the world that would help, he explained, "Post the speed limit as eleven- and one-half miles an hour. Watch the result."

His suggestion was implemented, and all were rewarded by watching the incoming drivers read the sign, and slow as they tried to digest its fatuity.

⌒

I saw a magnificent example of capturing the attention in Peyton Young's first day at school.

He'd been engaged to teach Elementary Physics.

He was well-qualified in the subject but had never taught before. I asked if he would not mind if I sat in; my request, ostensibly an offer of support, also imposed upon him the added burden of an audition.

The boys, of course, were on the lookout, primed to determine, in this first interchange, the position he would occupy in their estimation until the end of time.

He introduced himself and asked what weighed more, a pound of feathers or a pound of lead.

The boys were well pleased, to find in him, in his very first moment, an object worthy of contempt—one so ignorant he did not know the joke was old of old.

One student volunteered the answer (the supposed ruination of the joke), that they, of course, weighed the same.

"No," Mr. Young said. "For consider that the pound of lead is not adulterated, but the feathers are weighted with various things. I name the ecocytes, parasites which feed upon the stem's pulp. These, of course, have weight.

"Consider also the feathers' layering, arranged to capture and hold that air which acts as insulation in the bird's flight in the cold altitudes. The air, as all air, contains moisture, which has weight. And the feathers are never free of dust.

"Air, at sea level, weighs approximately 14.7 pounds per square inch. Water weighs 8 pounds a gallon. The weight of the ecocytes and dust, the water and the air, though minuscule must be determined for an accurate comparison.

"Now we see that such accuracy must allow for subtraction of the non-feather material, the *apparent*, unconsidered weight of the feathers being insufficient for our comparison.

"To bring the actual weight of the *feathers* up to that of the pound of lead, one must, then, add more feathers.

"Failing to do so, we must say that the *unconsidered* pound of feathers weighs *less* than the pound of lead; and, so the answer to my question, 'what weighs more?" is 'a pound of lead.'

"Or, if, we wish to be more precise, a pound of lead weighs more than a pound of 'that which we call feathers.'"

There was a confused pause. The students, then, perceiving they'd encountered comic genius, hooted with joy, and Young proceeded to teach them elementary physics.

Young's phrase became the catchword of that year, e.g. "would you please pass that which we call the muffins?"; and Fossett brought the house down, in his welcome to our returning, victorious eight-man Shells Crew, with, "I extend to you that which we call congratulations."

～

I note that Young's figures on the weight of air and water are correct. He always expressed pride in his invention of the ecocytes.

～

It is said that when critics convene they discuss form and function, while painters talk about turpentine.

We Academics, like all trades, exchange information constantly. This is vulgarly known as "gossip." And gossip is the most efficacious way to transmit information, for what makes the brain more acute than the promise of the forbidden?

At our frequent Conferences we present and digest papers on the various quiddities of the Education Process, but at their conclusion and over refreshment we dissect the errors and faults of our superiors, the ineptitude of our inferiors, the current and degraded state of our working materials (children); and, the difficulty in raising funds.[26]

Chadwick related an educational conference which took place on the Santa Fe *Super Chief*, on his travel to Pasadena.

He was in the Club Car, that Rialto, reading, he reports, Xenophon, *The Anabasis*, and we must credit his report; though, human memory being what it is, the volume may have been one of the murder mysteries to the devouring of which he was attached.

A prosperous looking man of his age sat opposite to him, nodding that civil greeting, either an acknowledgment of the need of silence or the possibility of conversation.

Chadwick motioned the newcomer to sit and offered him a cigarette. The silver case, a gift from the Class of '22, bore our school crest in enamel. The newcomer asked if he, Chadwick, were associated with St. Ives, and a conversation ensued, the other man confessing himself, also an educator.

He was, he said, in fact the Head of his school.

What school? Chadwick asked, and was told it was the American Association for the Study of Mithra.

Chadwick, of course, was intrigued, and, "only with difficulty," suppressed his natural ebullience in forwarding information. "I, here, practiced an unusual reserve, withholding from him, a likely superior in this knowledge, my acquaintance with Persian Zoroastrianism, the adoration of Bel-Marduk, and the Roman Mystery Cults which sprang from these. How useful is the proverb, 'Do not speak Arabic in the House of the Moor.'"

---

26 "What Professional will tempt fate, envy, and borrowers by flaunting material success? Such, when it exists, is well known to his fellows, and they may be counted upon to discharge their envy and loathing through jocular reference to the offender's new building, newly tamed alumnus, automobile or cravat." (Hollis, Diary Entry of 26 February, 1951)

In any case, Chadwick found, as he listened, that the Mithraism of which the other spoke was of an order distinct from that known to him of the religions and cults of that name of old; and that the title of the school appeared to be nothing more than a flag of convenience for a Seminary dedicated to what Chadwick increasingly came to recognize as Devil Worship.

His *vis-à-vis* was well fed, prosperously dressed, and possessed of gentlemanly manners. It was obvious his Academy was doing well. If, then, he were deranged about Religion, Chadwick concluded, he possessed a fine business sensibility.

Seeking to avoid an argument about Faith, "One of the Five Forbidden Topics,"[27] Chadwick decided to discuss the more mundane and safer aspects of Institutional operation.

"I concluded that the fellow, though, to my mind, deceived, was yet, neither a charlatan nor a hypocrite. It seemed he fully believed in his faith and Academy. But what, I wondered, were they teaching, and could I enquire without arousing the fellow's umbrage—for he was, finally, as entitled to his beliefs as I to mine—adding to myself, as only Human, that half-thought addendum—'mistaken as they are.'

"Is it a Religion, I thought; and (more easily determined, and perhaps less productive of Sectarian Friction), is it a School or a Cult?"

Chadwick let the fellow talk, encouraging him with the odd innocuous question on the safe topics of Ways and Means.

Yes, it occurred, the man's main preoccupations were the collection of tuition—especially, fees for Extras, such as trips, entertainments, added personal tutoring, sports equipment, books, and so on; the badgering of Alumni for funds—that "pursuit of game more shy and cunning than the Chamois," the management of faculty and

---

27 Religion, Money, Illness, Love, and Servants.

staff, and the attendant and constant squabbling over salaries, vacations, perquisites, and duties. The fellow, once started, was hard-put to curtail his plaint.

Chadwick opined that the man, being a Devil Worshipper, baulked of that release common to and beloved by Educators, the Bi-Yearly Conference, was delighted to find, if not a sympathetic, then a receptive ear.

Chadwick *was*, in fact sympathetic, for the fellow's practical problems were common to the two.

How, for example, to strike the balance between necessity of attracting many paying students, and the advertised benefit of the status offered by admission to a selective institution? (This ever the quandary of the Elite school. See *The Illusion of Scarcity*, Citation.[28])

This, the problem which cannot be aired "Among the Gentiles," occupied the Mithrist, as it has anyone selling anything. The struggle between educators and their potential consumer pool eventually devolves—in one generation or two, but inevitably—into a fight for the high ground: the high ground, in this case the right to *define the service offered*; and, so still not only complaint but inquiry on the part of the financially obligated.[29]

The fellow complained of the decline in the basic education of incoming students; the dedication of the teachers; the price of gravel for the walks; the wretched quality of that now offered as chalk, paper, pens, ink; the parsimony of potential donors; and the unfortunate current absence of devotion to education.

He, in short, transformed the journey into a two-man Educational Conference, at the end of which Chadwick found himself in total sympathy with his Brother Educator. He concluded that

---

28 Citation lacking. Ed.

29 This quote was beloved of Chadwick who, through his vast reading of pulp fiction, delighted in describing his profession as "a con-game." Ed.

the Mithraic Academy was, of *course* a school, and that, by exten-
sion, the Study of (that called) Mithra perhaps had as much claim to
legitimacy as did new doctrines both eventually discredited (eugenics or phrenology), and later accepted upon their own definition
[Christian Science, Mormonism, or indeed, (he wrote), some two
thousand years previously, Christianity].

"No," he wrote, "the fellow was running a school, it was dedicated to the promulgation of Religious concepts, and however they
may have differed from my own, the *culture* of the school (a creation
and amalgam of Human Beings constrained to 'get along') would
there as probably as here, inculcate the moral virtues of cooperation,
obedience (if not reverence), and diligence.

"Now I will widen my argument, as is my wont, past the point
of utility, and suggest that it is perhaps the *nature* of the School
which is the school's most effectively communicated precept"
(Richard Chadwick).

A LEGAL OPINION

The back (the East) side of the Red House has always been the butts to both the Rifle Range and the Archery Lanes.

The rifle butts were so-placed, not in deference to the sun, but in homage to the School's one martial artifact: the scar of war left by the Minié ball fired by the escaped Confederate Prisoners of Fort Lewis (1864), as pursuers mustered from what was then the Town Hall.

The Hall was purchased by the school in the expansion of 1892, with the stipulation that the Town would be the School's tenant, until completion of the new Municipal Buildings. Their vacation, of course, delayed by the insolvency of the following Panic of 1893.

When the town's Municipal Building was opened in 1896, three miles to the North, the building, now housing our School, was known locally as the Old South Hall, which name it retains to this day. Many a new (and old) resident, ignorant of the name's derivation, though curious, occasionally ask, as the building sits on the Northernmost part of the Campus, "South of *what*?" And here we have the answer.

We may see the building's original history preserved in the reverse-painted glass sign (circa 1869), "Town Clerk," now framed and hanging in the Bursar's office; in the location of the buried Minié ball; and the scars in the door frame of the Rear Entrance lintel, inflicted by the shot and sabers of those Confederate Soldiers escaped their prison Stockade at Fort Lewis.

They had overpowered their guards, old men "dug-out," and returned to the Union Colors, who had survived, variously, the Indian Wars, and the Mexican War of 1835, now in Civil Life, too old to fight in the National Conflict, but retained as part of the State Militia.

The Confederates, in their escape, had killed two men in their sixties, Thomas Finch, a farmer, and William A. Hayes, the town's leading carter.

Hayes had been a Sergeant Major of the 7th Cavalry in the 1850s where he had perfected his knowledge of the handling of horses. This, on his retirement and return to Fort Lewis, served him well in the acquisition and the training-up of stock and care of stock.

His profession had made him a wealthy man.

He had tried to re-enlist in 1861, but was rejected on account of age. He called in favors of sufficient weight to have himself commissioned a Major of Zouaves[30] (Reserve), and ordered a complete set of uniforms of his own design, which he was used to wear, displaying the boots (in red leather) and the spurs of a Cavalry Officer, which he was not, but which affectation was accepted by all as an excusable mark of Regimental Affection. he also wore the short, Ames, Officer's sword (now on display at the United States Cavalry Museum of the 3rd Armored, at Fort Hood), and a Kossuth, or "slouch hat" after the fashion adopted by the admirers of General Grant. (Both non-regulation with the Prescribed Uniform of Zouaves, *itself* rather romantic and outré.)

The escaping Confederates took the Burnside muskets of the slaughtered guard, Finch, and Hayes's Whitney revolver, highly engraved and chased in silver by Tiffany's of New York.

---

30 The Zouaves were volunteer Regiments in the Civil War. Their name and exotic uniform taken from that of the French Infantry of the 1830, serving in Algeria. Ed.

It was a Minié ball from the Burnside which creased the door of the Town Hall.

The escapees, it seems (wrongly) thought that the Town Hall must contain the jail (it did not), and, so, arms and ammunition.

In the event, the only weapon there was the shotgun owned by the Town Clerk, Matson, found there not for defense but for the hunting of waterfowl. He killed the one attacker and held the other at gunpoint.

This man was bound, and guarded, under the protest from the Townsmen, who wanted him killed, until surrendered to Army custody.

The town feared that, according to the regulations concerning Prisoners of War, the Rebel, the killer of Hayes and Finch, would simply be returned to Military Imprisonment, and perhaps escape— escape being a recognized responsibility of the Internee.

But feeling ran as high against him in the Army as it did in town. Hayes was respected there by officers and men alike. And the killer's sentence might have been a beating and a return to the stockade, but he was apprehended wearing Hayes's boots.

The tribunal ruled that this constituted "dress in the uniform of the Opposing Force," and that, thus, this man would be treated not as an escapee but as a spy.

The Prisoner was flanked by two corporals, the Court's President gave his verdict, and the Confederate was taken out, tied to a stake, and shot.

The Minié ball from the firefight is still discernable, buried in the oak of the Hall's back door. The sword is, as stated, in the Armor Museum, the engraved Whitney Revolver has vanished into the mysteries of Time, The Case's precedent lives in the judicial writings of Mr. Justice Gannett of the Massachusetts Supreme Judicial Court (associate Justice, 1928–1938. St. Ives, 1881–1885) and is enshrined in the Minority Opinion in *Korematsu v. United States*

(1944), the (unsuccessful) suit of the Japanese-American Coalition seeking relief from the distress of their Wartime imprisonment in the Internment Camps.

The Court rejected the plaintiffs' request for Certiorari on the grounds of lack of jurisdiction—the claimants having been adjudicated Enemy Combatants (which they then were not), and, so, not entitled to Constitutional rights of American Citizens (which they were).[31] Their claims, under the Fourteenth and First Amendments were rejected as their (adjudged) Combatant Status abrogated all rights under the Constitution; and they were, thus, "relaxed," to the care of the War Department.

The dissent of Justice Jackson concluded with a reference to the 1891 suit for damages by the widow of that John Cornel MacGuire, Corporal, Confederate States of America, who had been executed, at St. Ives, as a spy.

The defendant in that case was the State of Massachusetts. The plaintiff was represented by George William Gannett. He spoke of this loss on his promotion to the Supreme Judicial Court, and his speech was quoted by that young man who had been his Clerk, in 1928, now, in 1944, on the bench of the United States Supreme Court, writing in dissent, on Korematsu; Justice Jackson.

"Law, tortured into the service of passion is savagery. It destroys its victims, its proponents, and the very name of precedent."[32]

The 1944 Supreme Court decision still stands, but so, also, does the clarity of Jackson's dissent, and of his debt to his teacher, George William Gannett (St. Ives, 1881–1885).

---

31 The great majority, though not American citizens, were legal resident aliens. Ed.

32 Hollis originally quoted Jackson's dissent at greater length. He excised a portion in the galleys. It may be found in the Appendix. Ed.

THE USE OF TABOO

Jellicoe always encouraged (though he would never suggest) the reading of the *Arabian Nights*. His students, matured into his disciples, and, then, as the Faculty, periodically suggested including the book in the curriculum. This Jellicoe vehemently opposed: "They are full of bawdy: heitaras and eunuchs, epic copulations, and much description of and commentary on the female anatomy. Were such a book to come, officially, to a boy's notice he would shun it for life. No," he said, "dismiss it euphemistically, and keep it under lock and key. You may inspire a boy to be an Arabist, and even to learn locksmithing."

So the nature of the book was alluded to in various ways by The Head, the first recorded instance being in Chapel (Spring 1885):

> Those of you given to hunting may know that at twilight our sight fails. Our night vision, never very good, at twilight does not yet exist at all, and we cannot accurately perceive shape; but we can perceive movement.
>
> Nature has gifted us with a protective device most useful between day and evening. This is our *peripheral vision*, an extra-added perspicuity existing to alert us to danger around us.
>
> So, to aid our vision in the low and falling light, we need only to move the head, slowly, left to right, right to left, each new field revealing, as we traverse its periphery, the slightest movement.

But we must never look *directly* at that object drawn to our attention—it will vanish. We must look to one side.

Consider our Lord, Jesus Christ. We, who are given the opportunity to know Him personally may also learn *of* him—the second understanding, perhaps, leading to the first, more intimate Communion.

Let us turn to the written history of The Church, The Gospels; then to the teachers, Saints, and Martyrs of the Church, whose thought leads forward from the Gospels (as Theology), and backwards, in Philosophy, to our Mother Religion, that of The Jews.

By comparing our current understanding to that of our pre-decessors we may learn to appreciate it more fully. Not, perhaps, and if this is Heresy, forgive me—in the excellence of its wisdom, but in appreciation of its construction, as our understanding of the Roman Arch may lead us to wonder at the genius of the flying buttress, which, for the benefit of Catton, Major, and his team, is not a maneuver at football.

We may gaze straight on at our Church and learn many things. But a glance askance at a phenomenon may reward us by increasing our wonder.

And how much more askance than a book, first, of another culture; second, of another religion; and, lastly, of a nature foreign to us not only in its thought, but in its morals?

I refer, of course, to the *Arabian Nights*. Written, originally, in Arabic and Persian, and translated, these last six hundred years, into many tongues.

These are the fantasies of wonder, yes, containing djinn, Evil Spirits, ifrits, talking beasts, flying carpets, and bizarre denizens of other, imagined worlds.

We find here, also, human beings in all variety of sinfulness. Here are heitaras, which you students of Greek will understand to mean hired women; concubines, harlots, castrati, African servants of huge anatomical proportions; rape, incest, bestiality, and all of the sins attendant on our mortal state, awaiting only a moment of our inattention.

The book, though translated into modern languages, had long been accessible (in its most complete, which is to say, licentious, state) to our Puritan Western Mind, only to those versed in the Classical or Semitic Tongues, or in its necessary cleansed or bowdlerized versions, fit for a Christian's consumption.

Now there is a new English translation,[33] this great work of imagination marred by the re-inclusion of those passages any of reason must find objectionable.

Readers might find the licentious passages interesting as anthropology and, looking to one side, perceive the way in which the Islam of that time differs, and in what way perhaps is similar, *structurally* to our Modern Christianity.

(From *The Serial*)

Jellicoe continued, expanding the conceit with a homily on the essential unity of human nature, "the superficial differences in culture merely underlining their shared attributes, as, see, the Wolf and the Dog. Well and good; but, perceiving the similarities, one would be well-warned not to pet a wolf. And we, likewise, are well advised to avoid the, no doubt attractive, attractions of the Forbidden—for when are such ever proposed, save in the name of Reason?

"No, Passion causes the 'light to fail,' as light fails at dusk. The light is Reason. As it diminishes, we are incapable of distinguishing between good and ill. Until our eyes become accustomed to the

---

33 *The One Thousand Nights and a Night*, trans. Richard Burton, 1885.

failing light, we are well-advised to *look to one side*, which means to look away.

"I speak as you know, as one Master has discovered, in the luggage of one of our students, just returned from England, this book, *The Arabian Nights*, which I have, and I will say 'for his benefit,' confiscated, and placed where it will do no harm."

Modern readers, steeped in the rubric of psychology and psychiatry, may conclude that Jellico's "attempt at misdirection," "laid it on a bit thick."

But we must recall that he was speaking to boys, to late-adolescent boys; and to those who, as all boys, thought themselves, if not more wise, then certainly more cunning than their preceptors.

He occasionally kept the (supposedly) confiscated book on the work-table in his study, and many a boy stole a moment, at Tea at the Head's, to search out the illustrations. The volume was, more usually, locked in the study bookcase, its embossed red Morocco cover tantalizingly visible just beyond the glass.

His master stroke was to place, unannounced, a *second* copy of the book under Anthropology, in the School Library, there to be discovered (as of course it was) by one, and then by all; each swearing the next to silence, then, admitted to the secret; many discovering in the forbidden text, a love of reading.[34]

---

34 Jellicoe reports that at a conference of New England schools (The Five Brothers), a fellow headmaster, (DELETED), had discovered, during his years in Paris, the essays of Clerambaut (a contemporary of Charcot), on the prevalence of some latent paedophilia among educators. Jellicoe replied that he was well aware of it and found M. Clerambaut's assessment overly restrained. This, the reader will have anticipated me, leads us to the subject of the ANNO HORRIBILIS. [Bane referred to it (op cit) as "the year which dare not speak its name."]

Attempts at suppression or dissimulation here, as always, inspire contemplation of the offending material. (Clerambaut, *Le Sens et l'Anomie,* 1768: "The behavior of human beings when faced with power may clearly be observed in the higher primates. It is, there sexual in nature; the inferiors male and female, offering themselves to the more powerful males — the impulse, here, automatic and irresistible.")

Any organism of long-standing must, of course, experience change.

It is tempting to name this change progress — change for the better — but it is, perhaps more useful to consider it as decay. "For it may be true of bones that 'it is always stronger at the break,' but it is not true of organizations: for hypocrisy and that sanctimony born of shame may as easily be the product of trauma as may the true self-examination and repentance. Indeed, we know that the former case is the much more likely.

"What, in fact, is less likely than true repentance, which demands the sacrifice of that most precious of fantasies: that of one's essential goodness?

"One recognized the necessity. And He committed himself to suffer on our account. *But not in our stead.*" (Jellicoe, 1902.)

THE GAME

"Intention and Dedication are All—if the definition of All is 'an honest attempt.' If, however, the goal is other than mere 'trying,' it is probably good to consider strategy." (Coach Hardy Steffens, St. Ives, 1923–1950.)

Given the two forces equally matched, that of superior will is the more likely to prevail. But evaluation of "will," must, of course, be subjective, and will be most easily decided by historians, ascribing its possession to the victor.

These may also happily accept the charge of determining "material equality." For such, between two combatants, will never be equal, and will always be varied, as will its determination. For if both wealth and intention were equal, if determination could be so-judged identical, according to one moral standard, why in the world would there be conflict between two entities? There, would, then, in fact, be not two entities, but one, equal in prosperity, identical in philosophy, and with neither reason nor urge for competition.

Happy and underemployed reforming educators have recently suggested that games breed the urge for conflict. This is a late-appearing instance of meddling, the charm of its foolishness all but eclipsed by its destructiveness. Are boys to be deprived of fun and exercise because some insulated fool has misunderstood Plato?

For games, among boys, the education of whom is, after all, the point of the school, have been observed, by any who cared to watch, to divert excess energy into outlets not merely non-destructive, but creative; physical health, the formation of team-spirit, the love of demonstrated excellence, self-respect, and so on, those lessons bred into the bone, and so, surviving past all remembrance of European History, Literature, and other mixtures of fact and opinion.

One Educator, at a recent conference (DELETED), suggested that the Tug-of-War, that ancient inter- and intra-mural contest, be retitled The Tug of Peace.

Tolstoy wrote that when many remedies are proposed for a disease, the disease is incurable. Additionally, we may observe that, alternatively, such a disease may be imaginary. (nb. The Pageant of Psychoanalysis.[35])

Just so, the current fashionable "reconsideration" of sports is not an attempt to cure a problem, but to cure a solution. The examination of this misguided jollity may yield some useful insight.

Consider two opposing teams, pulling on a rope, a game pacific creatures might rename the Tug of Peace.

At the conclusion of the contest, what will the stronger team have demonstrated? That *their* vision of Peace (the game's title) prevailed over that of their opponents? This, is, of course, the definition of War.

To name war "peace," is a strategic move intended to confuse, demoralize, or co-opt an adversary, or to win to one's side, a weak, distracted, or undecided opponent, or potential ally. The attempted inculcation of confusion, then, may be signal warning (to the wary), of the stealthy operation of an opponent inviting an unconscious acceptance of the actually debatable proposition as the shortest path to peace.

See, not per contra, but in fact, in support, the "pep rally." This is an enjoyable form of propaganda, our efforts there in propitiation of the God of War. It is a prayer for Victory in Games, this Victory,

---

35   D.H. Wincott, 1941

as that in War, bringing with it an absolute, objective end of strife, and, so, peace.

"Peace" may also be found through submission, which, in the case of games, is called "defeat"; or in subjugation, and surrender, which the Pacifist understands as "victory." In these there is nothing to bar the Pacifist from declaring Victory at will, and without further effort.

All the above states are, of course, temporary, for the only total peace is in the Grave. Victory and vanquished, pacifist and warrior, tug of war, and tug of peace, all are the progress of Sisyphus. There is no human completion which is final, those offering the same will be found on the continuum of fools, ideologues, purveyors of snake oil, and the thugs and dictators who supplant them.

A sporting event is not only a contest, but enjoyed vicariously, a celebration of the essence of human life, which is, within and without, the play of antagonisms.

We at St. Ives have always considered sports important as exemplars of the difference between accomplishment and failure. We have, from the first (see Jellicoe), discouraged participation in those sports involving a subjective determination. We prefer, for example, swimming to diving. The ruling of a judge may be (overtly or silently) disputed. That of a stopwatch cannot.

In the days when we maintained the stable, the boys competed in horseracing and jumping, but did not compete (although some trained) in dressage.

"We have attempted to carry the lesson over" (in Jellicoe's phrase), into consideration of those contests the outcomes of which are necessarily the result of opinion, e.g. the debating society and its doppelganger, the study of Law.

Here we teach that *no* judge is impartial. In any human affair. That the Honorable are those who strive for impartiality, who are aware of the potential for both prejudice and inclination, acknowledge that to *identify* them alone is difficult, their eradication doubly so. These might act, then, with a measure of humility, prepared to temper justice with mercy not only as a moral but as a practical tool useful to decrease the likelihood of miscarriage.

Sports offer a handy yardstick for both teachers and students. Teaching the difference between opinion and fact. One has or has not scored a goal—just as he has or has not mastered differential calculus.

Outcomes which can be altered by "special pleading" (by recourse, that is, to a judge or panel) are likely to involve not only further error, but the exploitability of error to the benefit of one of the parties (plaintiff, defendant, or judge).

Such is inevitable in human interaction. In law, in politics, and so on. The educated may recognize the difference between fact and opinion, achievement and status, and, so, find self-worth when— inevitably—forced to choose (at some cost) between the two.

Strategy, as we learn through sports, is the ability to anticipate an opponent's operations, and order one's forces to exploit his weaknesses while concealing or otherwise minimizing one's own. It must begin with a concise statement of goals.

The nation whose goal is to "secure peace between two warring entities" will always be defeated, one or the other (or, indeed, both conjoined) dedicated to eject the foreign interlopers.[36] For the former struggle has no objective test of victory; and, given the lack of a goal, all strategy becomes a subjective entertainment.

That contact sports are currently disparaged as promoting violence is a late-appearing sign of a declining culture, self-hypnotized by prosperity. We see this, in the realm of Foreign Politics, here, the noble proclamation that we would be better off if we all just "got

---

36 "Or, indeed, by a conjunction of the two." Thoughts on Indochina, Hollis, essay, unpublished, 1964.

along," which is to say, if the culture momentarily holding the megaphone simply shared with the ignorant world its perception that "we all want the same things," and imposed that perception upon them.

("We will leave to one side the Civil Suit, the business dispute, the marital strife or divorce, and the knowledge that even dissention at the Quilting Bee will occasionally devolve into unpleasantness." Moore.[37])

~

During my two years at Oxford, I discovered and enjoyed the current European craze for Psychoanalysis.

We, especially, the Returned Veterans, took to this new toy as subsequent generations would embrace communism, or eugenics, or, indeed, Vegetarianism: as a way to assert intellectual superiority through what would, absent the grand imprimatur of Science, be recognizable as a parlor game not dissimilar to Anagrams.

For, of course, it was a game, and all the more delightful in that we, its players, participated not only in the play, but in the formation of the Rules.

For what else was (or could have been) the constant, the Talmudic, presentation and partisan championship of the various schools. The Versailles Peace Conference was mocked for occupying itself with prolonged discussions on the proposed shape of the table. How much more absurd (but no less enjoyable), "bull sessions" disputing, not the nature, but the *name* of various supposed properties of the mind, their provenance, differing strengths and possible conjunctions? Those who spoke German had a decided edge in the Game, but the works of the Major Authorities (Freud, Adler, Jung, Reik, to name a few) had, at that time (1919) all been translated

---

37   In correspondence, date lost.

into English. These were adduced, each by its adherents, exactly as, in the Twenties, individuals would champion the various creators of Contract Bridge, adherents proclaiming his particular expert the sole source of wisdom.

Some few of our group had actually begun Psychoanalysis, and only the limitless human capacity for gullibility prevented us from observing that, absent their enthusiasm, we could discern no change in behavior, nor—a much later realization—that none was in fact required. But we read the books and knew the words, and enjoyed fitting them together in our own minds, and, more importantly, communally, during the Oxford evenings we devoted to the subject's discussion.

Over a protracted period, having seen men blowing each other apart for no discernable reason, I was not inclined to take seriously a straight-faced devotion to the consideration of childhood trauma as the source of human dissatisfaction.

Those in Analysis, I observed, *could* not "get any better," as no one could describe what "better" meant.

But Freud wrote with wit, and simplicity of human folly, substituting for the notions of sin or demonic possession a psychological disruption. A distinction without a difference, as far as I could see. His observations were sound—that we act from motives hidden from our consciousness; and that an examination of thoughts and acts may help us to identify those motives; but though the theory was demonstrable, it had no demonstrable therapeutic effect. The analysand, I saw, enjoyed the process (as who would not, licensed to complain, to fantasize, and to suspend social norms of speech), as one would a séance—which the psychoanalytic interchange essentially was—contact being made not with the-Dead-Who-Still-Live, but with its identical twin, called, here, The Past.

In a subsequent attack of hobbyism[38] I found that Buddha had anticipated Freud, thus: "What does a man smile at? What does he frown at? Man cannot hide himself."

Freud's useful accomplishment was to bring the verity of an Inner Life, once again, to the Modern Mind, while both the Industrialists and the Bolsheviks were insistent on returning to a strict Materialism.

"What does it make you think of?" "Tell me your dream," these phrases seemed (and seem) to me, the reduction of Psychoanalysis to its primal roots (and those most useful): the enlistment of *Imagination* into self-knowledge. The discipline was not therapeutic (who has benefitted from it?), but it was provocative.

(See also, the Victorian embrace of Philology, and Comparative Myth: Good for what? Good as they passed the time, harmlessly, in mental exercise.)

Psychoanalysis, I concluded, was a game.

Well, I believe in games, but note the inevitable misuse, if they are not so-labeled.

What is their correct use? The happy expense of energy, in individual or communal effort to achieve a stated goal, *of no further worth*.

---

38 Hollis's, unpublished, "Oriental Religions," existing only as a few pages of holograph notes, Private Collection.

THE ST. IVES GAME

Our Game, called, by the Town, but never by us of the School, "The St. Ives Game," evolved, it is fairly clear, from the efforts of the first few years of Boys to clear the South Field.

New England rocks, as we all know, spring from the earth as the dragon's teeth sown by that Proto-Down-Easter, Cadmus.

We know Jellicoe put the boys to work to build their mutual Establishment; many an Old Boy, in his mémoires, refers *first* to his experience of *building* the School; *most* of those reminiscences beginning with an anecdote of clearing the field.

Jellicoe turned the clearing of the field into a contest (or the boys did so) and these ab-originals, strutting their primogeniture, passed the competition along to new arrivals.

The Field was, of course, eventually cleared for construction of the Hall (1881), and the Game migrated to the Athletic Field, where the Five Balls replaced the rocks, and its evolution and elaboration, began. The new boys came each Fall, the rocks each Spring.

You, the Readers, all of whom are acquainted with and most of whom have played the Game, may detect here my Freudian comparison of its development to that of Neurosis, or of Culture; and, perhaps, my suspicion that the two are one.

I was privileged to play off-forward in the Game, during my last two terms at School. That I treasure the approval of my School Teammates more than any academic honors could be disbelieved only by those who have never played team sports.

ADMISSIONS

Many said they were on the field at the death of Tom Fraser. Many more claimed they had seen his body, borne in on the gymnasium door, or had looked on as Dr. Moss worked on him, the door laid over two pews in the Chancel. (We know the poem.)

Some few, of course, were there. A somewhat greater number heard of it that afternoon, their memories over time, of course, amending or embellishing the actual fact into myth. "The wise man discounts the tales of others, the true sage disbelieves his own." (Tacitus.)

The School is deeply indebted to the Fraser Family for Fraser Hall; and, as we know, for the (originally anonymous) Endowment establishing the Marigold Scholarships, the list of whose recipients would indeed grace any institution.

Sufficient time has passed since its inauguration to call attention to the earliest reasoning in the Scholarship's award.

First, it has always been, and remains, open to any young man between thirteen and eighteen years of age.

He is required to submit a brief (and, until recently, hand-written) essay of not more than 500 words, about himself, and his reasons for seeking admission to the school.

He was (until quite recently) *invited* to attach a character reference from a clergyperson, teacher, athletic coach, or mentor. This— to share a pedagogical secret—was not to determine his qualities (anyone responding to a request for endorsement will, of course, assert the petitioner's excellence), but to gauge the applicant's ability to follow simple rules.

"Write your five hundred words. Enclose same with your supporting letter in" (this practice still exists, now treated simply as "tradition") "a *brown*" (emphasis in the original) "manila envelope, 9x12 inches, including a self-addressed, stamped *brown* envelope of letter size, and a handwritten note (by the applicant), asserting that he has assembled the package himself."

The process, then could assess, *practically,* the ability of the applicant to follow instructions *in pursuit of a goal.*[39]

The application process was not intended to determine his "level of academic achievement"—any child of moderate intelligence can master the eight years of the three "R's" in two or three months of work; nor to gauge his "Scholastic Aptitude" (whatever that may mean), but to assess the one thing: did he want to come here sufficiently to overcome the near-inescapable adolescent lack of concentration (of old called "dreaminess") and the resistance to authority (the concomitant of the yearning for independence) inevitable on the approach of manhood.

Many of the early applications were of a severely limited vocabulary. Some were the compositions, it seems, of a near-illiterate. But the only applications rejected out-of-hand were those which were illegible.

For anyone could be taught to read and most to write concisely, but a boy who could not determine the connection between his

---

39 As the, now discontinued, requirement of the hand-written essay determined, practically, his ability to be neat and precise. I was always astounded by the amount of applications submitted in an envelope other-than-brown. These, invariably, contained an essay declaring the writer's burning desire, indeed, his need to attend St. Ives. I was often asked to suggest the reason for our school's demonstrable success in selecting good students. I always credited the brown envelope.

essay's legibility and the attainment of his supposed goal could not be taught to reason.

We could not (and can not) determine if a boy "wants to learn," and so chose to rely on a mechanical test. We were thus, as in the example of swimming and diving, preferring the decision of the stopwatch to that of the judge.

Was this process imperfect? What human operation is not?; but the experiment has prospered, as has The Fund, and the extent of the awards has, for a long while, been limited but by the ability of the school to discover teachers meeting our requirements. (Given sufficient funds—which are provided—we may always build more classrooms. But to what end?)

∾

The identity of The Fund's founder had long been conjectured and was the subject of rumor and unfounded, but believed, "report of the knowing." It was not revealed until the 1950's by Priscilla Rogers Witt (Fraser), who remarked that the benefactors could have been identified by any of the residents of Point Reyes, where the Fraser family summered, and where Tom kept his racing skiff, *Marigold*.

THE BIBLE

A mention of the Frasers must bring me to the subject of wealth and power, which, in any case, are one; and, of course, to philanthropy.

The March family were (one can hardly believe that it now has to be explained), among the Harrimans and Huntingtons—the earliest of Railroad Barons.

They owned (and their heirs now own) a large amount of land in Northern California. This is a remnant, for they, in the second generation, donated five times the current acreage to the Federal Government for use as a National Park.

And see the fame gained on our Playing Field, by one of their number, a member of a collateral branch, the young James Jerome (St. Ives, 1902–1911).

We read in *The Serial* (#85, June 1909):

Those who are conversant with the Bible are aware that our right hand should not know what our left hand doeth. This, generally understood as an adjuration to anonymous philanthropy, was interpreted last Saturday, by our young Jerome, in a new light. He, in an outburst of inspired and original exegesis, standing in Left Field, and underneath that "pop fly," his catch of which would retire the side and secure for St. Ives Game Nine and the Series, fumbled and dropped the ball, allowing our opponents to score the tying run. And had that not sufficed, he also botched the throw to Home, inviting St. Jude's Cronin to score from

Third, to win the game. And so the Trophy rests, for one more year, at St. Jude's in far-off Connecticut.

We may only hope that next year, should March, then a Sixth-Former, yet again adorn our Field, he will have abandoned his Bible Studies.

In the event, the Bible quip proved intriguing, if not prophetic, given James Jerome's career, first in the Church, and, after his conversion, in the Priesthood—a progression (to those who knew him here), in which the second term was less shocking than its predecessor.

For many a boy—I am tempted to say every boy—longs for certainty and order, and this, coupled with a youth's love of renunciation has ever led young men into the Church, as into the Armed Forces. Mature success seems to all but the few cursed with early fame, an impossible accomplishment—the various recommended paths to which appearing both arduous, and, were that insufficient, unattractive. But renunciation is open to all and may be performed in the instant of decision.

Athletics offers benefits both obvious and subtle.

It is clear that victory in sports is enjoyable, as are the status and camaraderie of a group endeavor, as is that rivalry, which is a healthy release of aggression and, at once, a training in ambition. To the athlete, effort brings reward, irrespective of Victory.

Participants—win or lose—improve their bodily health, and, thus, clear their minds. And they learn not only that loss does not equal death but that it may inspire to renewed and perfected effort.[40]

---

40 From the address of Monsignor James Jerome, S.J., to the graduating class of 1949:

"My awkwardness and inattention on the field destroyed our hopes. I was prepared not only to slink away, not only to retire from school, but — you young athletes will credit it — to end a life whose shame would admit of no remittance.

Father Jerome also noted that defeat in sports acted most differently upon the spirit from defeat in business, and the wider world—that in sports the chastened competitor first vows not what he intends to do to his opponent at their next encounter, but what he intends to do with himself prior to it.

Hardy Steffens, "Coach Steff," to those generations who revered him, was asked by Father Jerome after his speech to account for the ability of sports to teach its lessons so frequently where both academics and religion had so often failed. Why, for example, was the parable "the other cheek," so clearly stated and so seldom practiced in life?

"Received religion is very well," he said, "but on the field and in the locker room, we're teaching a different understanding of the other cheek. Not to turn *away,* but to think *ahead,* so that the *next* time they don't get hit on the cheek the *first* time" (Hardy Steffens, St. Ives, 1923–1950).

"But see, as our bleachers emptied in sorrow. My teammates approached me. I foresaw either their silent scorn, or, worse, a killing commiseration.

"But they, in their rough-mercy, as one, picked me up, carried me to and threw me in the Willow. When I emerged, they did it again. And repeated the process until they had discharged all their wrath. Then they chaffed and embraced me. I will never forget it."

THE DROWNED MAIDEN

The Ghost in the Hall was always understood to be a drowned maiden.

She was, depending on the period, understood to be the daughter of: an ostler, a village mechanic, a travelling magician (my favorite); later, of a chiropractor, and currently, I am told, and hope this does not indicate a vitiation of a Myth's romance, a radio repairman (with no aspersion intended upon that craft).

I note the choice, on the part of succeeding generations of boys, of the father's profession, each signaling distance from and some inferiority to those understood as permitted to gentlemen.

Here we find, thus, the "poor but honest" young woman, specified as an exemplar of a "class not our own," and, so, exempting, by implication, the daughters, mothers, and wives of our own class from any possibility of moral negligence.

The young girl's ghost persists, bound to this world, as she died unshriven, drowning herself rather than facing the shame of unwed pregnancy.

She had been betrayed, of course, by her betters: a young Teacher at the school.

He, then, *was* and *was not* of that other group of Riperians, the boys, who, in keeping her memory alive, were her defenders.

Who else would defend her?

Not the Administrators, to imagine whom as ardent creatures would be a vile exercise.

Perhaps the Teachers? In union with that "young master," one of their own? But they had grown out of the fantasy of youth into unquestionable adulthood. The myth was not their possession, but the boys'.

And they imagined "the Young Master," unnamed, as possessing not only those good qualities the individual boy might award himself, but those the boy longed to possess and emulate. For, in telling the tale were they not "the Young Master's" doppelgangers? Of course they were, which may be proved by the fact that they never blamed him for the girl's demise.

There he was, imagined: handsome, virile, young, romantic, Byronic, in short; rich, cultured, and reserved, but lured beyond resistance by the young girl's virgin grace. A sinner, yes, but one who, I remember being told, distinctly (a young boy then myself), sinned from love.

He and the girl had met, fallen in love, courted discretely and chastely, and vowed to marry. The lad was called off to War, and the two, borne on the waves of their mutual passion, had consummated their love in advance of the formalities.

His father, I recall, was opposed to the *mesalliance*, but the Youth knew that in time, as he came to know the girl, he would accept her as his daughter.

This was the myth I heard as a student; the Young Man, then, being called to service in Cuba or Manilla.

When I returned as an instructor, I learned that the young man's marriage had been interrupted by his enlistment in the A.E.F., and service in France.

In any case, he died in battle, and the girl, as before, bereft, unmarried, and pregnant, drowned herself in the Pond.

But why had her ghost chosen to haunt the Hall? Why not the pond itself; or, for choice, the Boathouse, then, as now, a lonely and romantic spot?[41] Why had the ghostly Evening Mists proved insufficient to induce her Spirit to stay put?

But no, the drowned girl haunted the Hall, and had always done so; and many was the boy who rose to fame recounting his experience of her Spirit.

Its appearance was (and, I hope, remains, should the Legend happily persist) announced by a "slight chill and a stillness in the air, and a feeling akin to but different from anxiety" (See: *The Sentinel*, Autumn Term, 1951).

After this, all witnesses report the vision of a young female form, clothed in white, her progress closer to floating than to human locomotion, moving across the doorway to the Arch. Always at Dusk.

Her appearance, in some renditions, was matched to the phases of the Moon, in others to the supposed date of her soldier-love's demise, or to the date of her death.

That her name was unknown was accounted, I recall, as simple courtesy to her virgin state and reputation.

We boys, then, were her *chevaliers*. Our fantasy granted us the pride of manhood without the adolescent fear of or ambiguity about sex. For didn't the Soldier's lust, and his failure at its control, however sanctioned by Love, lead to the demise of this perfect (as unknowable) creature?

And so she haunted, and I hope still haunts the Hall, providing, as must any myth, that instruction which (as tradition, gossip, or

---

41　From *The Diaries*, September 12, 1965:
　"Rereading the new-published '*Recollections*,' it is obvious that *The Boathouse* would be excluded from this myth of sexuality and virginity; possessing its own myth, or, say, better, legend, as that place where, this or that contemporary bragged he had taken some Town girl.
　"Did this occur? Perhaps, but I doubt it; for the Town practiced its own restriction, its admonitions, requiring no myth for their support."
　The following line has been effaced.

forbidden knowledge) is the most effective medium for the transmission of values; the moral imperatives here both "protect virginity"; and, I think, "Do not mix town and gown."

But, again, why the Hall rather than the Pond? (For the myth always specifies the Hall.) Or, to invert the question, why should the ghost inhabiting the Hall be that of a young woman?

As I write it becomes clear that the only nubile women to which the boys were exposed, during Term, were, of course, the Hall's serving girls. And I recall my own schoolboy fantasies.

The utility of the tale, then, may be understood as a warning clothed as a ghost story, the warning recasting a moral or cultural restriction as a primitive Taboo. For though the boys were lustful, curious, and anxious, who among them would want to have congress with the Dead?

I note also that the myth includes, as a matter of course, that the young teacher served when called, thus buttressing another aspect of the St. Ives ethos (that of military service); and that, finally, I saw the ghost myself, in Christmas Term, of, I believe, 1913.

DOUBT

Dissolution is sown in Conception. This is the essence of the seed, that it has been born to die. Its destiny was writ not in the moment of its birth but when Being emerged from Time, from the Time before Time, or from nothing very much at all.

So say those hailed as brave philosophers. But what say the rest, whose embrace of Nothingness began not in Eternity, but at some school.[42]

For if all we can perceive of the world is all we can know of it, our understanding can only be mechanical: that fire burns and ice cools, each but fulfilling its physical nature—a tautology.

But what, then, can we know of sin, who will not acknowledge the metaphysical, which is to say the Soul? And if Everything came from Nothing or had Always Existed (which are two ways to say the same thing: that "it is beyond our comprehension"), what can we say of guilt and shame, save they must be mere adaptive mechanisms, and love but a procreative tool in order to ensure our species' survival? To what end? To none?

My argument may of course be dismissed as specious if finally reduced to first principles which, as they cannot be further reduced, can only rest upon a mutual acknowledgment of definitions: that justice, love, beauty, and truth exist.

---

42 "Here called Agnosticism, Nietzscheism, and so on." (Found in the original ms. Ed.)

Of the last, note that the atheist becomes metaphysician in his appeal to Truth as, *prima facie*, proving as absurd that some entity called God created the world. Why is this to him absurd? As he perceives that all things have a natural cause. By what organ does he perceive this? Through the operation of reason. Point to it, he cannot.

The Teacher, mentor, the Housemaster, the Head, in any institution of a religious bent is constantly reasoning with the boys who have discovered Doubt. And how much better to address it in the safety and security not only of a school, but with the assurance that adolescence will neither harshly punish nor overly challenge the heretic.

"Go forth and sin, then," is a handy phrase. "Take what you need from your fellows, steal the school car, kill those who stand in your way, and take your new knowledge to the World, scorning their stupid qualms, which can only be cowardice."

GOOD AND EVIL

It is held that we are divided according to our opinion of human nature, one moiety holding its essence good, the other evil.

A more accurate view may be that the divergent opinions do not constitute two different groups, but are present, not only serially but simultaneously and always in each human breast. (For what could the always convinced, not to say vehement, assertion of one over the other indicate, but repression of the recognition of contrary examples?)

One who performs an act of surpassing humanity we call a hero, if he does so continually he is called a saint.

All admiration, then, contains the opposed understanding—on the one hand that the mass of humanity is flawed, on the other that we have the potential to overcome our defects.

The very act of applauding courage, certainly, contains a measure of impertinence; as, I believe, someone observed.[43] Recognizing the superiority of the hero to the mass is, of course, to recognize his superiority to ourselves, the pain of which may be expunged by our generosity, called "praise," and, so, our self-awarded superiority to the mass, in our quality of Commentator or Critic. This is the situation which Fossett compared, in his 1928 Prize Lecture, to that of the "Anti-Stratfordians":

---

43   It was Joseph Conrad. Ed.

Those inspired to attribute the authorship of Shakespeare's works to someone of their choosing, other than the Bard, illustrate our endless human capacity for cunning.

Stunned by a facility of invention beyond their ken, they obviate the, to them, noxious necessity of admiration, and, so, of any true humility, as a challenge to their lack of self worth. This intolerable affront, the ever-plastic mind transmutes into a hardy arrogance. Viz:

"Shakespeare did not write these plays. Who but a fool would mindlessly award to a fraud the mantle of genius? My superior understanding, however, may salvage, for the World at Large, something of worth regarding this oeuvre." *This, in its only less virulent, but more widespread presentation, we may recognize as the opinion of The English Teacher.* (Emphasis added by Hollis. Ed.)

It was this lecture, which, when republished in the *Journal of New England Private Education* (November 1929), led to that "revolution in Pedagogy,"[44] known, now, more familiarly, as THE ST. IVES SYSTEM.

The term "system" itself, as Fossett wrote, is another assertion of The Repressive Instinct's "right to be heard." (op cit.)

"There is no system. Rather, just the observation that there is no need of one, and, so, no possibility of corruption-by-authority of the unregulated interchange between author and reader, which is not only the chief delight, but the sole purpose of literature.

"Future generations of Educators will inevitably elaborate this observation, each personal scheme an attempt by the newly inspired to express both his understanding and appreciation in abstractions returning literature to the care of himself, the pedagogue.

---

44 Citation lacking. Ed.

"Yes, but," Fossett continued, casting himself into the role of that yet-unborn new generation of revolutionaries who, in every time and in every appearance are inspired to point the unobservant the way toward savagery, "Yes, but . . .

"I do not understand what is meant by 'the teaching of literature' where, pray did Boswell or Johnson, Swift, Pope or Hazlitt, or, or, or . . . Where did they study? And where were the instructors and the schools generous enough to devote themselves to the explication of *their* texts to an ignorant public? And as such schools did not exist, who bought the books? And who enjoyed them?"

Fossett's argument, of course—and, as he wrote—would hold no weight with the "disciples of Disciples." (What pure inspiration survives attempts at its transmission? None.)

It was inevitable that even here (why should we be exempt?), classes in English Literature should evolve from those informal talks, eventually codified as "Discussion Sessions"—the euphemism announcing, as all must, the presence of an underlying obscenity.[45]

"Ask a boy what interests him. Learning this, suggest some two or three books he might find diverting. If he has difficulty reading them, direct him to the dictionary for questions of fact; or to you, for (lacking another word) those of understanding or interpretation. Meet him regularly to 'hear his views on life.' *Never correct them.* Neither 'test' him, as if you were a licensing authority. Leave that to the bureaucrats he will encounter when he leaves, and until his death. We have the Opportunity, here, to offer him something else."

"Yes, but, what if he will not read?"

"In that case," as Fossett said, "punish and shame him."

---

45 Courses in English Literature appeared at the school as early as 1950. Prior to this, many recall that delightful informality we were to ascribe to Hollis's years at Oxford and his oft-proclaimed affection for its Tutor System. Ed.

PHILANTHROPY

I am told the open stacks persist at St. Ives. The "discussion groups" have inevitably, degenerated into Survey Classes in World Literature, overviews of this or that, with essays demanded on theme, structure, and so on, teaching the young to mimic pedantry.

"Ah, well," we say, "some New Voice will emerge, some iconoclast, some inspirational magician, some second Fossett."

It is not impossible. But not here; or, if here, not for long, for either he (or, increasingly, since 1958, she) will tire of the school's strictures and culture, or the school Governors, some generations removed from inspiration, will weary of impertinence.

I asked Dr. Fossett about the Term System, the "open shelves," and the Head of House Organization. He replied that yes, our school owed a debt to his experience of the English Public Schools, but that his true Road to Damascus moment occurred, ironically, in Jerusalem.

Prior to taking Orders he had conceived the plan of a year's residence there, in a Rabbinical Academy to perfect his knowledge of Biblical Hebrew—that, of the three classic tongues in which, to use his words, he was "the most deficient."

There, at the school, the Yeshiva[46] Ben Yehuda, he found not only Jews but Christians of many denominations, and instruction taking place not only in contemporary Hebrew but, for the benefit of visitors, in that German which was, at the time, the language of

---

46 "Seminary," Heb. Ed.

advanced Biblical scholarship, which language was well known to Fossett, as part of any higher education in those Edwardian Days. (See Fossett's comment on the replacement of the German language by that of the French, as the *lingua franca* of enlightenment, "An Irony, surely.")

The first text studied contained two Hebrew words with which he was unfamiliar.

At the lecture's conclusion he sought out a dictionary. He found none, and asked the Professor (the Rabbi) to translate for him. He then asked for the location of the dictionary and was told that for the first year they wouldn't be using one, and that if he sought the meaning of a word, he should, "ask someone to aid you in your inquiry."

I recall a visit I made, in 1936, to Los Angeles, with Fossett, as his Dogsbody. (I am reluctant even now to use the word "protégé," but it seems that was what I was.)

We got down from the train, began to walk, and were quickly "turned around." ("Lost," is the Anglo-Saxon word, he would have admonished me.)

We were on our way to dinner, at the home of Mrs. Prudence Lovell, whose support for the school, then, required no introduction, and which today is memorialized by the Lovell House. Fossett had been told that Mrs. Lovell's home was a five-minute walk from the Station. The fatal words, "you cannot miss it," had been spoken, and Fossett had lost the address, remembering only that the street had something to do with Oaks.

Here he brought his study of Hebrew into play. For the first street encountered on leaving the station was Allen Street, and Fossett recalled that Oak in Hebrew was Alon.

Pleased with his mnemonic, demonstrating not only sagacity but study, we spent much of a hot morning, in fruitless search up and down Allen Street, for the large White Colonial, with the green shutters which we could not miss.

Heat, thirst and fatigue found us at a luncheonette, where Fossett placed a call to the Lovell residence.

From Fossett's address, that night, to the California "Friends of St. Ives":

I was correct in my recollection that Alon means Oak in Hebrew. My self-congratulation marred by the discovery, in my phone call, that the Lovell House, was, indeed, but three minutes' walk from the station, but that the station was that of Pasadena, not in Los Angeles, where we had mistakenly detrained.

The Pasadena street name, was, we know, indeed connected with the idea of Oak, being named, Oak Street. Where we now find ourselves foregathered to discuss Education.

I will, prompted by my morning's adventures take as my text, "If a Little Learning is a dangerous thing, what may we not allege of its surfeit?"

∾

(Note: The following was excised from the 1965 edition, it is included here rather than in the Appendix, as it is, uniquely among the deleted material, *the continuation* of a Chapter. Ed.)

We were in Pasadena, of course, in search of philanthropy, which is to say hunting for money.

This is the dark secret of Private Education: that longevity and success breed expansion, which must be supported by the enthusiasm and generosity of Alumni, but that their enthusiasm and inspiration not only outstrips their support, but that any support comes with the baggage of the donor's "good ideas," implementation of which, of course, costs money, thus, the tightening "death spiral."

And so, the School, as any organization, is run to death by its own hounds, supporters suggesting elaboration, and the market demanding that the school supply it, or lose market share to proliferated imitators able to provide (or claim to provide) a similar service at a reduced cost.

The law of life is Grow or Die. Merchants may fund growth by borrowing or floating stock. The school must fund its growth (and, so its life), by what, finally, must be acknowledged as begging.

We know The Bible cautions that rather than admit appetite in the House of the Wealthy, it were better to cut one's own throat. The successful school, however, and, most especially, its Head, must do the first, and cannot do the latter.

And so here we encounter that "Mating Dance of the Peacocks," a full description of the horror of which would require a better hand than mine—the incisive irony of a Mark Twain, perhaps, or the lavish love of wonder of Burton's translation of *The Arabian Nights*.

Tumbler pigeons display and encourage availability through "tumbling" in flight. They fold their wings and fall backwards, twisting toward the ground in the most outlandish routines.

So it is with a Headmaster on his courting missions to the Alumni.

He must, at once, convince his quarry of two opposite and mutually exclusive propositions; that he desires funds for the support and elaboration of the School ("for The School's Honor," God forgive us), but that he, not being a beggar, does not *require* them, as the school is doing fine.

Is he, then, offering a service to his auditors? They, and he, must conspire to act as if it is so—that service which will reflect both status and honor upon the gulled (here, known as "the donor").

The school must never be seen as in grave financial difficulties, for what successful man (donor) has come to success through reinforcing failure?

What is on offer to the Alumnus? Honor, as above; and, in the major case, that status established through his apostrophization of this or that building or fund, and (at least to *some* extent) control of the same. Wherein lies the rub.

See here the mating dance. For just as the Headmaster must, in decency, clothe his rapacity, so must the donor conceal his desire for power.

Let us assume that each desires only the welfare of the school.

The Head understands the School's health comes from its sustenance, given which he and his subordinates will take care of the rest; the donor, especially him appealed to in (*absit omen*) calamity, wants to express his love in a re-organization of that entity now self-proclaimed as weakened by consistent mismanagement.

The school is suffering, and the businessman sets himself—as potential savior—to determine the cause. The cause is always financial imbalance. Now the donor is a busy man, it is beneath him and a waste of his time to consider the day-to-day expenses of a school.

Meat, heat, maintenance, the price of all these has risen, as has that of everything else in life. What is to be done?

Tuition may be increased, but a rise above that demanded by our Brother Schools may lead to a drop in enrollment.

Well, then, the businessman observes, we must widen enrollment.

Out comes the fountain pen, and we see, defaced, the snowy napery of the Fifth Avenue restaurant. If the cost-per-student-hour is constant, and the major expenses (salaries, as always) remains constant, the answer is plain.

It has long been the "cookie jar" of private schools to "sweat" the teachers, suggesting to them that if prestige will not fill the larder, it may make hunger more bearable. Let us, then, the Philanthropist says, either cut salaries, or, in increasing the enrollment, keep the number of teachers constant, and tell them to work harder.

But there is a limit to even the work of a slave.

This is the businessman's better answer: Tuition remains constant (this stasis advertised as a "source of Pride," and an evidence of disinterest). But the school must increase enrollment.

How will it be done?

Now the donor whom the tablecloth has proved correct, is in his element, which is arithmetic.

It seems, he says, that our school accepts only (we may fill in a percentage number, over the last fifty years it has averaged 28 percent) of applicants. Were we to accept (out comes the pen again) 8 to 10 percent more, why, the books would balance, and we would see a surplus in so-many years.

Above we see operations of that wisdom called "business sense." I should not carp. I do not have it. It involves a simple and blunt understanding of commerce, and I and our school have benefitted from it since our founding—as has any school. So I indict myself of arrogance.

How may one balance the books? One may always lower the quality of the product. We may water the wine and add sand to the sugar; we may lessen the quality of students, and/or that of their instructors.

These latter, should they stay, while sweated by increased enrollment, will have to work harder (with a not-unnatural resentment), and the students, even if not less intelligent, will be less well educated than now is the case.

The teachers will be taxed as their work load increases (the quality and quantity of students each changing for the worse), and, as their salaries will not increase, there will be resignations, which will, doubtless, require a lowering of our standards of employment, as we will then enjoy a reputation both for low pay and overwork.

"No, however," says our donor, "the problems of a school—being a financial entity—cannot, at base, be less soluble than those of a breakfast cereal company," and here our composite and imaginary friend may produce the second cigar, or suggest Port—"we find the crux and the base of the problem, and it lies in the reluctance of the theoretical to embrace mechanics.

"There are costs, there are prices, and there is income. One may reduce the first, increase the second, or put both to one side and increase volume."

I sigh and ask how we can do this without lowering our standards, and his answer, shorn of its cladding, is this: advertising.

Shampoo, I am taught, is sold not by extolling its ability to clean hair, but by announcement of its ability to impart "sheen" and "luxurious softness" or "caressability." It may also be advertised as containing any number of ingredients, standard, inert, or, indeed, imaginary, whose names may capture the imagination.

(Advertising, then, is lying? I ask. And he is stunned by a look suggesting in my question a fatuity equal to an announcement that fire burns.)

Is it a lie, then, I ask, that an education at St. Ives builds character? And he replies with the names of several of his school friends, whose lack of the same in later life resulted in notoriety.

He smiles, out comes the fountain pen, and I am invited, granted "visitor" status as "a Temporary Man of the World," the witness to the creation of a simple scheme to simultaneously widen enrollment and raise tuition.

The scheme is inevitably this: (and it takes, as its model, the marketing of the breakfast cereal):

Like those industrial grocers, we will enclose in our package a Special Treat or token or premium. The package in our case is education.

The makers of cornflakes will bury a miniature plastic boat or airplane in their fodder. *We* will announce various *special and unique* courses of study. Their irresistible novelty and obvious utility will compensate buyers handily for their additional outlay in fees.

The donor is but human, and, so his support for us, in our need, is contingent upon our acceptance and implementation of his simple schemes (or a simulacrum thereof; but woe to the man who is Found Out, giving short weight to his benefactor).

But, honorable men—so are we all, all honorable men—we, of the school, once having given our word, will obey the letter and the spirit of the gift, our desire to do right out-distanced only by our terror of discovery in malfeasance.

We might add to our particular product (Education) delightful treats, eg: school trips to this or that instructive location, lessons in Esperanto, Volapük[47], ceramics or fencing, studies in the History of Popular Entertainment, and any number of factitious but attractively untaxing pursuits.

We are free to name such elaboration a "new liberal view of the Education Process," or some such, relishing the discovery, old of old, that, with but a little hard common sense, something may be had for nothing.

But we must recall that the plastic sailboat cannot improve the breakfast cereal, it may only trick us into purchasing an inferior product. Why must the product be inferior? Why else the inducement? (It can only be inferior to, or, as in the case of Breakfast Cereal, at best, at parity *with* its competitors.)[48]

---

47 Volapük, like the better-known Esperanto, was a late-Victorian invented language. Their creators perceived that different languages reduce the ability of human beings to communicate, thus, that World Peace could be brought about by adoption of a Universal Tongue. The first Worldwide Conference of the Universal Esperanto Association was held in Basel, Switzerland, in 1908. The opening session was marred by a fistfight which broke out between the Belgian and the Portuguese contingent on the pronunciation of the language's motto: the Belgians holding to *oo Lingva Internaceo*, the Portuguese *oo Linguva Internateo*. Ed.

48 In which case to remain cost-competitive its package must contain *less* of the stuff.

Is this last the case with schools? Perhaps. If not, what have we to offer unique among the better schools? I suggest Tradition, and that culture which, working by stealth, forms the boy into the man imbued with certain first principles. These like those of the family, are no less real for not being expressly enumerated.

But the donor has finished his second cigar, and there is no need to elaborate his vision past the current glass of port. He has spoken.

And so, the School, now suffering from elaboration, as do all successful organisms (this suffering called, in youth Growing Pains, and, by the aged, damned Foolishness), embraces the most obvious solution: further elaboration ("Independent Study," "Credit for Life Experience," "Journal-Keeping," and so on).

This puts the problem at one remove, on the appearance of which remove it will be found to have grown geometrically (the rationally "innovative" school, having become a diploma mill), wherein we find, once again, the problem of the well-used hammer.

Its handle breaks, and is replaced. Later the head cracks, and we buy a new head. Is it now the same hammer? The question may be mooted at length by the theoretical, but I, in my years of tenure, had a school to run.

~

Well, each has to bring his pigs to market.

The addition of new Programs (under Brandt and Myself) previously unimagined by our Founders, might, by the more philosophical, be accepted as inevitable. There is, certainly, in this view, some admixture of cowardice; or, I, a craven, may propose "Quietism."

Jellicoe could not have foreseen the ubiquity of the automobile, nor the cultural changes it wrought, nor the constant drone of the radio's idiot blandishments—even, and perhaps especially, those presented as "information." If these have not lessened the ability of the young to concentrate, they have certainly affected their ability to concentrate on schoolwork.

New generations of students in this modern age have discovered amusement perhaps known to Ancient Persia, but forgotten in this Puritan Land.

To what unforeseeable ends has youth's assertive impulse progressed, from the Victorian Boy "Breaking Bounds," and perhaps smoking, to the temptations on offer, or, better say, forced upon the youth today?

The heart does not yearn for what it does not see. But the eye, currently, sees so much, through cinema, and hears that through the ether by which the imagination is enflamed. It is not cooled as is that of the young reader (of whatever romance), putting down his tale to discover himself still on the Library porch, his eyes refocusing on the peace of the Long Pond still below.

These are, you will note, the musings of a fool—as any but a saint becomes upon deserving the honorific, "an old man."

A SCHOOLMASTER

President Wilson was a schoolmaster, and a University Head. He possessed both those professions' signal faults of pomposity and insistence on obedience, to guard against which should be the constant study of the similarly placed.

Fossett had known him at Princeton. He thought little of him as a University President, and less as a commander-in-chief of that Army in which many of his students served and died.

Fossett did not and would not deign to adopt that outlook he termed "that fool Globalism." "The League of Nations," he wrote, "is, in effect, 'passing a law against Crime.' I having pledged my life my fortune and my sacred Honor to stand as a missionary among Criminals (the Boys). I knew the difference, as Wilson did not, between Boys and Nations. And I knew the similarities.

"'Greater understanding' between boys will not foster cooperation. Boys understand each other perfectly. They are a bunch of rowdy thugs. Greater *discipline*, the promise of reward, and the threat of punishment will conduce to peace among boys. So it is with nations."

But Fossett did see one good in Wilsonian Globalism. This he understood not as a panacea, nor as a specific but as an interesting novelty. (It was the Age of Novelties.)

Fossett's notion, elaborated from Wilson's bizarre, "untutored ignorance of the World," was that of a Sister School (of which notion he was most probably the originator). This twinning, commonplace today, was then a great novelty; and, first suggested by

Fossett, perhaps, as something between happy experiment and a harmless stunt.

His friendship with Morton Frees (later Lord Manning) led him to consider coupling ourselves with a school in that India where Frees had served, and to employ his Family's long connection there with Indian Education, especially their sponsorship of the Hindu College for the Advancement of Education, and its preparatory school, the Surat Academy.

We have certainly benefitted from this now long established cultural exchange.

I will name the presence here, during the close of my Headmastership, of the third generation of the Jaradi family; and the generous participation, on the Board, now, of the second of that distinguished clan.

The exchange of students in the Tenth form, of course, apes the old Roman custom of Guest Friendship. There, closely allied families "swapped sons," at adolescence.

I note also the healthy custom of the Latter-Day Saints of dispatching the youth for a two-year overseas mission. Does this foster Mormonism? I cannot say. It may or may not, but it certainly promotes maturity; for, away from home, the young man, like the Romans of old, must learn to be respectful, be thoughtful, and careful both to observe and to adopt the customs of the elders around him. A good working definition of maturity. These Missionaries, on a return which may or may not have increased adherents to their Faith, will most certainly have increased their own abilities to serve it at home.

Surat, of course, is famed as the diamond center of India and in 1938 the Diamond was added to our school crest in compliment to the Surat Academy. (The Crest, now, "Argent, a Wolf's Head, Gules, erased; in Fess, a lozenge, sable Propre." Translated: on a silver shield, a red wolf's head, surmounted by a "black diamond.")

The Black Diamond is the stuff of legend, that form so-beloved by Jellicoe, for "Leavening the mundane 3 R's with Fantasy." This Jellicoe named as the truest challenge of the schoolmaster. How rare is that ability—the perfection of the "necessity to inspire?" I have never possessed and have always reverenced it.

The diamond itself was, of course, the gift of his Excellency Sir Rajit Singh, KCMG, the Marathata of Rampore, on the graduation of his son Ghotal,[49] from our school.

The stone has acquired histories and mysteries, accreted and perfected through the late-night gossip of those generations of boys, the elders avowing to the newcomers the truth of the sole, the only, accurate true and awful, the murderous and no-doubt erotic story of the Diamond's provenance.

The stone itself appears to be a dark-blue square cut diamond of approximately seven carats, of "the first water." Such a stone, at its market price today would fetch, I am told, easily one million dollars.

But is the stone real?

This question has been asked since its appearance at St. Ives; and here we find the wisdom of Fossett, in following the insights of Jellicoe regarding fantasy.

Fossett would not have the stone insured, for to do so he would have had to have had it appraised; and had it been found—as he suspected—to have been mere paste, or a lesser stone dyed black, its worth as a talisman would have been destroyed, as would the pride of that friend to the school, Sir Rajit Singh.

So it rests today, as it has since the graduation of Prince Ghotal Singh, in the vaults of Shreve, Crump and Lowe, in Boston.

It was transported thence, after its presentation, from the school, by Charles Crandall (St. Ives, 1914).

---

49 Note, later, Captain Prince Ghotal Singh, King's Kyber Rifles. Ed.

He wrote (Private Correspondence) "I took one last look in wonder, in surrendering the stone, at the request of the Head Cashier whose task it was to verify the contents, before the box was wrapped and sealed."

I will always wonder if his astonishment was due to the diamond's stunning worth, or its obvious falsity.[50]

---

50 The gift was made with the stipulation that the diamond would not be sold for eighty years after its receipt. Captain Prince Ghotal Singh, K.K.R., fell to the Japanese in Burma, in 1941.

ROMANCE

Jellicoe and Brandt shared a hobbyist Orientalism no doubt inspired largely by *The Arabian Nights*, and hardened through that Anglophilia which, however we might deny it, may be found near the root of all New England Private Education. For, from whence but Eton, Winchester, and Harrow would we have taken our models? These, mixed with the individualism of the old New England one-room schoolhouse, have given us St. Ives, and our Brother Schools.

Our alumni and veterans, of course, credit the second influence over the first, and may allege that the quiddity of our ways comes not from the desire to inculcate Class Consciousness, but, rather, through molding the young mind upon those stoical forms open to both us and our Transatlantic Cousins.

Perhaps.

And perhaps we, here, have been spared the ethnocentrism masquerading as ecumenicism which, though it may have been prepared by the Public Schools, flowered in the British Foreign Service, in the (choose one or both) administration or subjugation of various Foreign folk.

We count ourselves, no doubt, in inescapable self-delusion, as "downright"—decent Americans, New Englanders, Christians, and so on; and perhaps we are some or all of the above. But though we may descend, on the Distaff Side, from the Country Schoolhouse, we also inherit the New England tradition of the Age of Sail, and the grand- or great-grandfather, uncle or great-uncle, who shipped before the mast, and whose memory is preserved in the Chinese Gong, Ivory opium pipe, mahogany case chronometer, carved elephant tusk, and so on, still in many a Best Parlor in our New England homes.

The study of Foreign Customs, called, variously, Ethnology, Sociology, Anthropology, Comparative Sociology, Comparative Mythology, and so on, may approach, I suppose, toward Science; but how much better to have experienced these differences in fiction; or, for the most fortunate, around the Round Oak stove, as Tales of the Foreign Land.

How many a boy was taxed to get his eyes back in his head, the blessed after hearing, and the rest after reading, these fantasia? We recall the boy's delight in *Moby Dick*, *Martin Eden*, Marryatt, Burton, and so on; and, in poetry, the work of Kipling, long a favorite of Brandt, who preferred him over all contemporary poets, much to the amusement of the cognoscenti of that day.

But Kipling's poetry holds up, when the taste for Whitman is, to a modern mind, incomprehensible.

Brandt loved to read of romance, and said that when he could no longer find it in teaching he would "retire the birch rod, fold my tents, and slink away."[51]

I recall how he would flavor the most mundane of observations with comparison to the exotic. It was a pose, as we all knew, and the glint in his eye left us no doubt that he, himself was privy to the secret. But it was delightful. Imagine "the smoke from a

---

51 A new boy asked Brandt how long he had been studying history. Brandt said fifty years. The new boy said, "You must know things that never even *happened*." Brandt said, "Indeed I do."

Connecticut Valley Factory laying low over the river, 'like the fug in an Opium Den.'"[52]

I recall one of the evenings in the Common Room. Teachers were, of course, invited, to this best of symposia, as were members of TOP, and returning Alumni.

The topic, as always, came around (if it had not so begun) to education—for that was the interest of Brandt's life, and he, co-heir to Jellicoe, had convened us there.

"I'll tell you what it is," he said. "It is footbinding."

Brandt, here, proceeded to reduce Comparative Anthropology to words of one or two syllables.

"Why is the Chinese Woman's foot bound? To constrict her movements. She is, thus, in the same boat as the Victorian Spinster: she has not married, she cannot live alone, where can she go? She must stay home and serve.

"Is this system monstrous? We today unanimously affirm that it is. And brought to acknowledge such, we see it begin to change, in Woman's Suffrage, Education, Employment, and so on. But what, in our experience, might it resemble?

"Say we take a young soul, and hobble it to an institution where, to survive, the local ways must be learned. We may call this a prison or a school. In either case, the sum of the oral and written Law is called Culture.

"We may experiment with thinking less of Education, inspired, perhaps, by the too-frequent repetition of unqualified and sub-jective goals: to 'prepare one for life,' to 'socialize the young,' 'to broaden ones outlook,' to 'expose one to Literature or Art.' But why do we mouth these vagaries? If we heard them hawked at a

---

52   From *The Serial*, Spring 1935. "Memories of Brandt, by 'Ptolemy,'" Harrison Johnson, '21.

Carnival Ground, would we not smile at human gullibility and move on?

"The gull of Modern Education may be proud to pay a fortune to have his son taught the useless, the pointless, or the imaginary, as it displays his status, in displaying waste.[53]

"But this 'course of study' also binds the boy into a community of the like-minded, and the similarly constrained. His choice of profession is now limited. He may be a doctor, lawyer, Military Man, Cleric; or, *perhaps*, an accountant or dentist; but he will never learn a trade or craft, and will, in fact, starve before stooping to work as a cobbler or plumber, let alone to menial labor. He may, 'go slumming,' in a *wanderjahr*, as a hobo navvy, but he must always return to the society obedience to the rules of which he imbibed during his school years.

"What is the cultural purpose of this bizarre custom—of training up the young like an espaliered plant, and calling it education? What, to our Society, is the *use* of this elite schooling, or is the answer contained in the phrase?

"If so, then, the phenomenon must change as economic conditions change, and we may see the Five Brothers, and our Olympian English Betters, fade from the industrialized land—schools like ours being found, by a later day, odd—and, perhaps, unfortunate— as the institution of the Harem, which, let us acknowledge, though it may have some benefit to its proprietors, is, finally, but slavery to the inhabitants, however well-provided for.

"We cannot 'teach the Young to Think,' nor 'Widen their World,' nor 'Expose them to the Arts,' through these things may occur independently of our best efforts. We *can* teach them to read, write, and to do sums; teach languages, and music; and they,

---

53 See *The Higher Learning* by Thorstein Veblen, 1914, its original sub-title "A Study in Depravity."

for their part, may learn if they so-choose. Let us remember to leave the promise of the unquantifiable benefit to the hucksters of Breakfast Foods and Automobiles; and, so, do as little harm as possible, always, *always* doubting ourselves, and 'not only our methods, but our motives.'"[54]

---

54 Harrison Johnson, op cit.

AN ANTI-AIRCRAFT GUN

Explanations are better than instructions, in that they do not so easily trigger the human resistance to correction.

Superior to both is the facilitation of understanding without conscious knowledge of its transmission—or, in English, knowledge imparted by a teacher which the student feels he has arrived at independently.

At Messines we had captured a 20mm German Oerlikon cannon. This was their automatic-firing Naval Cannon, adapted to anti-aircraft.[55]

The gun was far superior to the hand-loaded, slow, and low-powered pieces used by our Field Artillery; it was, in fact, the bugbear of all Allied flyers on the Front.

A Boffin, Garrick Fry,[56] attached to the Armaments Establishment at Whitfield, was dispatched to oversee the dismantling and transport of the captured gun to Bologne, and, then, to England, for evaluation-and-reverse-engineering (copying).

Heavy bombardment had interdicted the rail lines such that we were not only rather hungry, but had run out of ammunition for

---

55 Excised from original: that cannon's full name. Offering some wry amusement to the troops, was *Oerlikon Contrives*, "For Use Against Birds."

56 A Boffin is a civilian scientist. Garrick Fry, later, Sir Garrick Fry, was knighted in the Second World War for his work at the Royal Aircraft Establishment in development of ordinance, famed for its employment by "the Dam Busters."

the field pieces which were our only defense against the German bombers.

The Oerlikon was captured with a large store of its ammunition, and, so we trained it from West to East, and began popping merrily away at the German Aircraft.

We did not possess the gun's manual, but our Boffin possessed a keen mind and a slide rule. He observed the fall and the fruitless detonation of the proximity shells, questioned our perplexed gunners, and examined the machine. The use of its dials for the adjustments for windage and elevation were clear, as was that for rate-of-fire.

But there was one extra dial the use of which was *not* clear, and it was to this, of course, that the Boffin's attention was drawn.

In the three days of his visit he noted the varying degrees of error in our gunnery, and, in a burst of inspiration compared them to his observations of the barometer; and hypothesized that perhaps the differences in trajectory were due to air density. Then, if I can suggest an explanation of thought processes I can only otherwise characterize as "genius," he guessed that the mysterious dial might be a correction for barometric pressure, a difference in which would indeed cause a variation in ballistic trajectory.

A turn of the dial resulted in a minute depression or elevation of the gun barrel, and he seemed to have solved the problem.

The greater problem, as he later explained, was communicating his hypothesis to the Gunners. Why on Earth, that is, would they listen to one who was not only a Civilian, but a Boffin, any observations of whom must be dismissed with amusement, and, if continued, stilled by a professional contempt for vile impertinence.

Meanwhile the German Albatross[57] were flying, unmolested, to do great damage in our Rear.

---

57   A German fighter-bomber, first flown in 1916. Ed.

The Sergeant-Gunners were cursing the Hun, the Oerlikon, and every last thing on God's earth, with language of which the "sanguinary" was the least of the adjectives.

And they were having a cup of tea.

Our Boffin sat with them and accepted a mug.

"Funny thing," he said, "*I* just learned it, last month, from my Aunt.

"If you look at the tea you see bubbles in the mug. When they're in the *center*, that mean's High Pressure; around the rim, *Low* Pressure. I've been watching it since I learned the trick, and it works. It's a Barometer."

"What's it good for?" A Sergeant said.

"Well," the Boffin said, "*one* thing: she said, it's good for this: she noticed that, when she threw the ball for Prinny, *High* pressure days, she'd have to throw it harder, to have it cover the same distance. Air Density or something, I'd expect."

He sipped the tea. His left hand, on the mystery knob, turned it, idly, and the gun barrel rose slightly, and fell.

"Hey, don't muck about with that," the Sergeant said.

"Prinny's my Aunt's poodle," the Boffin said. But the Sergeant had already taken out a pencil and a notebook and was making calculations.

The Oerlikon was put into action, now, with great results, downing several of the bombers. In their absence, the reconstruction of the rail-lines, and the reestablishment of service, allowed the gun's removal to the Rear.

Explanations are more effective than instructions, and the ability to incite intuition is, for the teacher, the highest skill of all.

I, who observed the events, always felt that the Boffin's mechanical understanding of Instruction was laudable; his inclusion of the Aunt and the poodle raised it to the status of True Art.

FIRST DO NO HARM

"We had momentarily exhausted the dissection of that Run in Question," Chaffers said; holding, as he always did, against the Huntsman's ineptitude.

"A new bottle was brought. In the pause as it was opened, the fellow Blunt brought up from London noted its date, 1881.

"'This puts me in mind,' she said, 'of a famous case of that year. Have any of you heard of the furor in Chancery over the question of Primogeniture in Crown v. Panton?'

"'By Jove,' Rosemary said, 'If you cannot discuss horses, have the common decency to hold your tongue.'"

From *Col. Rosemary's Conversion*, by
Harold Ross-Merry, London, 1893

Solomon, in that best of all Old Man's books, wrote that all is Vanity. This is neither more nor less untrue than the youth's uttermost article of faith, that all the Old are fools.

An honest disquisition may be attempted by *one* of two disparate groups on the subject of their conjunction or opposition.

Such examination of relations between, for example, women and men, Black and White, Christian and Jew, can only be written, however, by a member of *one* of the two groups. However, he may try to understand, and so bridge, any divide, his understanding can only have been formed in the group by which he was raised. He may accept or reject these views, to the extent they are accessible to him, but he can never—however he acts—be free of their influence. Any work on bridging these divisions can be parochial or even-handed; each of the two choices being, however good-willed, finally, an example of conscious or unconscious but unconquerable prejudice.

But consider Age writing about Youth (and what else is the Study of Education?). Here the aged assume the gap comprehensible, for we have *been* young. I wonder.

The Luddites, rick-burners, Rousseauvians, and modern practitioners of Permissive Education hark back to pastoral times, when the young could, perhaps, be left free to learn from nature, their acculturation into Society accomplished by the necessity of communal labor on the Land.

The Land, then, and the family, were the school of the pre-industrial age, during which age no one outside of the Religious clerisy found it necessary to ponder upon Education.

Now the agricultural life is past, the tutor and the one-room school are themselves replaced by that called An Educational System, taking, increasingly, those orders from the State it once took from the Church.

The profession of Teacher persists, but it is not unlikely that it will soon be considered as vestigial as the buggy whip sockets found in the early automobiles.

Chevening wrote that organized Education in America existed first to educate Clerics, then, as access to it widened, citizens, and then, with the growth of technology, workers. And that its final iteration, before its demise, would be to train slaves.

I am glad I will not be here to see his observation proved or disproved; for I've happily reached that final penultimate of Maturity, just prior to senescence. Grown past both anxiety and curiosity about the Future, I no longer can be brought to care. I was given a life to live, and I am grateful to have lived it with what I hope is but a modicum of trouble to others.

Finally, I learned some few things, but I am not sure they have a name. The same may be said of the things I taught, if, indeed, I actually taught anyone anything.

The mastery of objective subjects may be accomplished with more ease from a book than in a classroom; and that of the subjective is, finally, just a matter of opinion, leaving under the head of Education but Example. In this I hope I have displayed a preponderance of honesty, kindness, and a humility not totally hypocritical. In any case, instruction and study, conjoined in my leisure and career as Education. And it was under that title perhaps not more false than most, that I lived my life.

~

Some hold that the waning of desire makes room for wisdom, but I have never seen a fool mature. These, alone, among all human sub-divisions, seem doomed to happy stasis.

And why—even should they be so-inclined—should they change what is a position of some power for the indecision and the give-and-take of healthy communal life? I do not see why. Nor do they.

Folly, however, is sometimes difficult for the sentient man to recognize, which is the operative mechanism for his subjugation by both the Confidence Game and the bait-and-switch of Politics.

Yet each must bring his own pigs to market, even should those metaphoric beasts be the commercial life of an educational institution.

I note the aligned inability of Youth, full of desire, and a not irrational self-importance (are they not, in their era, the transmitters of the gene-pool?), to distinguish, in the aged, folly from—if I will not say wisdom I will say a considered conservatism.

Tradition and myth go far in shielding the institution from Radicalism, and one can, indeed, observe the Grand Hailing signs of Jacobinism and its ensuing Terror when Traditions are discarded or mocked—the eternally new discovery of the Avant Garde.

The grandfather has run his race. He is happy to discover this last period of novelty and joy: watching the young thing emerge.

Free from the necessity of instruction and discipline, disabused of their efficacy, and well aware of their potential and his own for harm, he is enthralled by the realization that he may withhold comment, and, so, judgment. He may likely conclude that, had he done so as a parent, the results of his guardianship, if not better, would certainly have been no worse.

Smollett wrote that the opinions of the aged expert are likely to be received by the young practitioner with derision. For the old man has tried, discarded, invented, and perfected years of theory, reduced by the affront of actuality, into a few common sense principles.

He, having grown past not only reverence for but memory of received theory, is, in fact near-incapable of delineating his thought processes for the benefit of the young. He has progressed beyond thought-processes, into that simplicity in its final form, perhaps resembling Hinduism or Buddhism. Is it not so?

The phrase "first do no harm" is often misattributed to Hippocrates, but it is not found in his Oath.

It precedes him and is timeless is the best precept for the teacher, who may not know how to aid, but, if only of moderate imagination can see what will injure the young persons in his charge.

A love of the phrase came down to me through Fossett, who had gotten it from Jellicoe, who quoted it regularly, and never without a smile.

Fossett asked The Head why he smiled and was told a story from the Civil War.

Jellicoe had served alongside the 15th Massachusetts. They had received conflicting orders, which brought them late to the Second Battle of Bull Run, arriving at its conclusion.

It was then suggested that their Regimental Motto, "Liberty and Union," be changed to "First Do No Harm."

"We should beware of too much erudition," Jellicoe said. "What harm may it do? I'll tell you." Here he pointed to the old ridged scar in his right cheek, which he always called his "dueling scar."

"We were in Bivouac around Harper's Ferry and the men were drinking, I was one of them. One of our Sergeants had invited a member of the 15th to our improvised Mess. The beer had run out, when one of the men produced a jug of moonshine, uncorked it and began to drink. The Sergeant of the Second asked if it were drinkable, and our man said 'Better not to chance it,' corked the jug, and added 'First do no Harm.'

"The offended Sergeant drew and cocked and shot his Navy Colt, but his arm was knocked up, the shot went wild, and creased my cheek."

"Sir," Fossett replied, "I've also heard that you received the scar at Heidelberg."

"I've heard that, too," Jellicoe said, "it is a pity both stories cannot be true."

APPENDIX

The following material was excised from the 1965 Edition.

Some Recollections of St. Ives was privately printed, in an edition of one thousand copies. It was intended for distribution to the School's Alumni. There were three hundred Presentation Copies, in calf, the remainder, in half-calf.

The edition was printed, at no charge, by Treviss and Hilton of Boston, then under the direction of Mr. Henry Robison.

Mr. Robison was the grandfather of William Hilton (St. Ives, 1968), and an active supporter of the School. He took it on himself, as such, to remove from the Edition material he considered injurious to the School's reputation, doing so without either the consent or knowledge of the author.

From Hollis's response to Treviss and Hilton:

June 8, 1965

Sirs, The Bard has taught that when remedy is exhausted, so is Grief.

The book having been printed and distributed, I have no remedy. Were I more of a Christian, I would forgive both your temerity and your presumption. That I find the latter the more offensive may offer you a clue to my character, as your action has confirmed me in an opinion of yours.

—Charles Hollis, Private Correspondence

THE EXCISED MATERIAL

ANNO HORRIBILIS

It is obvious that human beings in disrupted situations will improvise and implement a social order. The survivors of the shipwreck, by means traditional and extemporized, choose a leader based upon their assessment of his ability to lead them to safety.

Less obvious is that all human society is always in some degree of extremity. See the savage facing wild beasts and murderous rivals; the agriculturalist contending not only with weather but the change in tastes, population, transportation, and government; the industrial society additionally involved in conflicts, civil or not, between labor and capital, and this periodically under the threat (perceived or ignored) of war. Culture is, even at its most peaceful, an attempt to create safety through unity.

The very question of armament in time of peace is a signal example of that fatal cascade of divisiveness occasioned (as with the savage and the beasts) by community reactions to threat.

Those societies last longest which can most easily identify threat and marshal (or coerce) unity sufficient to deal with it. To do so requires a leader both wise and strong.

How seldom is this combination found in, and even more rarely practiced by, one capable of forging unanimity by appeal to first principles?

These may be good or bad; founded on virtue or its opposite, but to succeed, they must be presented and accepted as beyond question.

I list: the Divine Right of Kings, the Will of God, Manifest Destiny, and so on.

These myths will be accompanied by a talisman claiming to be a codification, proof-text, or guarantee of Authenticity, and, so, indisputable and probative. I name the Bible, The Koran, Book of Mormon, the Constitution, the Hippocratic Oath, the 39 Articles, Marriage Vows, and so on.

What a precarious structure is Culture. It can operate only upon an acceptance so deeply embedded in the mind of the governed as to be—most usually—not only unrecognized, but, when recognized and examined, dismissed by elites (the product of cultural success) as heresy, their dismissal understood by them and merchandised as "the birth of Rationality"—that is, a peremptory challenge to culture.

Having discovered (accurately) that the marriage vow, the Apostles' Creed, the Pledge of Allegiance are based on Myth—the poetic presentation of a basic, unprovable, assertion—a New Man may declare himself freed, as might the recovered alcoholic.

He may reason, for example, that vows are not needed if we "simply love each other," private property and its anxieties banished if we will only "share," borders (and, thus countries) an obvious and dangerous incitement to war.

Thus the rationalist, barred from inventing the wheel, reinvents human society. He cannot bring this improvement about himself, so he bands with his fellow discoverers. They, however, find themselves at a loss, for though they clearly envision a new world of cooperation and equality, they find that they can only attempt to implement it among the not-yet inspired through some sort of coercion.

They are, thus, in the same position as the shipwrecked passengers. They must elect a leader. This person, modern history shows, will inevitably become a despot. For the visions of the Inspired can only be made flesh through unanimity, thus the unconvinced of a group too large for mutual interaction and resistant to a revised myth must be silenced or eliminated.

The nineteenth-century comedy contained the stock figure of the inmate, confined in a mental institution, who thought he was Napoleon. We laugh because it is true, we know him. For what do these modern Jacobins (Bolsheviks, Armchair Socialists, and Rationalists) imagine themselves to be except an omnipotent dictator, who, sadly, for the moment, lacks but an army?

It is no wonder that the prime exponents of anarchy are and have always been teachers. For we are used to the unquestioned assertion of power over the uneducated.

~

Physical abuse—until most recently—and paedophilia, eternally, have been the concomitant impositions of the immoral on those put in their care.

One must monitor the behavior of teachers more assiduously than that of students. The greatest responsibility of the Headmaster is to protect the second from the first.

Physically, first of all—as the current situation so sadly reveals. And philosophically—debarring the instructors from imposing their prejudices on the young. This must be accomplished through the creation and oversight of a Strong, Simple Curriculum.

How much of the Headmaster's job is the civil rejection of good, novel educational ideas?

~

To those who transgress the civil and the moral law, a swift denunciation, dismissal, and an absolute commitment to prosecution *in spite of the inevitable counsel to "consider the honor of the school"* must, unfortunately, stand in for the certainty of severe beatings which, of old, I am sure, aided many a challenged instructor to keep his wretched impulses in check.[58]

---

58 Found in Holograph in Hollis's Diary, see also, his testimony at the trial. The above was dated one year after the trial's conclusion from the week of the Funeral for the Victim, who had taken his own life. [His name never mentioned in the Criminal proceedings, or (though, of course, widely known) in the records of the school.] Hollis gave the funeral oration. It has not survived.

DAEDALUS

Mass delusion always presents itself as Revelation.

The Tulip Mania, the South Seas Bubble, the Ponzi Scheme, Faith Healing, the Stock Market Mania of the late-twenties, these appeared to the bitten as did the Philosopher's Stone of Old, or the Djinn's Lamp of the Arabian Nights: the instant solution to all struggle.

The Philosopher's Stone, the Holy Grail, the Shroud of Turin, possession of these required the effort of Search. But the Obvious Perfect *Notion* (as opposed to *object*), required no search at all: the solution to the problem of human toil had here been discovered and announced, and all one need do is accept it.

Freudian Psychoanalysis appeared in our American Scene in the late twenties, as an instant panacea, the perfection of which was marred only by the inability of the adherents and practitioners to actually name the ills it professed to cure. Disaffection, unease, remorse, depression, and other inevitable components of the human condition were now labeled, by those *au courant*, as illness called "neurosis." We were taught to believe that these feelings, suppressed, created *symptoms*, and that recovery of the trauma which occasioned the feelings would make the symptoms disappear.

Now, who would pay money to undergo this process with a Fakir in a booth at a State Fair? However, the mass delusion swept an Eastern metropolis, which looked down on the blandishments of Aimee Semple MacPherson as idiocy.

Freud's trademark notion was the Oedipus Complex. He held that this myth revealed the ineradicable human instinct of the Son to kill his Father.

But I have been a father and a son myself, and I suggest his notion was so instantly and happily embraced because it clothed not only a different but a less acceptable truth.

Here I will use a practicable idea of Freud's: that the unavowable may be inverted, victim and perpetrator, cause and effect, switched, to defuse the unpleasant thought.

What could be less pleasant than the thought of Patricide?

The question came to me reading a historical novel.[59] The author states, as a matter of course, that Icarus died, not because he *literally* flew too near the sun; but, that he, the apprentice to his father, the Master Artificer, surpassed him so conclusively in skill that his father threw him off the roof.

I received this with that feeling of disquiet which subsequent, inevitable attempts at denial could not suppress—a reliable indication of having heard the truth.

The myths of Parricide are few, those of infanticide abound.

The Myth of Icarus, by squinting the eyes, can be seen as identical with the Binding of Isaac—the latter, here made more horrible by the suggesting that the murder was God's will. Which leads one, in privacy, to a comparison to that most universal of Western myths, Christ's Crucifixion. (Here the horror is tempered, as in the case of Isaac: Isaac's death stayed by the hand of an angel; Christ by God's reward of Eternal Life.)

It may be that paedophilia, child abuse, corporal punishment, and, indeed, the infliction of boredom reveal the Teachers' impulse to destroy the perennial affront which is youth.

---

59 *The Mask of Apollo* by Mary Renault. Ed.

CO-EDUCATION

It had long been suggested—mooted first as a jest or novelty—that we admit girls to the school.

There is, of course, "no new thing under the sun," and this notion of co-education, as all must, had its antecedents. I name the attraction of novelty for those who mistake it for inspiration: See Feminism, Female Suffrage, the general and moral imperative to widen Opportunity; and the widespread love of Academics for a good quarrel.

My article in the *New England Journal*[60] gave rise to a question at that Fall's conference, and the formation of the inevitable "Study Group" to which it was my privilege, for my sins, to be elected.

My prejudice fell, as usual, on the side of conservative (or Fabian) wisdom: my position was ridiculed by the Jacobin elements (NAME WITHHELD) as: "Do nothing, and, when faced with the deleterious effects of inaction, do nothing."

But I do not find the slur, well-put as it was, deserved. For on my election to the Study Group I had put myself, as, if I may, a "counter-irritant," to study the question.

My family and I were down on the Island. I had the entire month of August before me. I would go to the Beach Shack every day, after my morning coffee, announcing "Well, I'll go to work," to which my eldest daughter, Pet, twelve, I believe, at the time, would respond, "night-night."

---

60 This source cannot be found. Ed.

For, yes, I employed not only that vacation, but most of my time at home, when not on the campus, in relaxation and rest, "and found nothing more restful than relaxation."

Over the years I'd interested myself in the life of Nantucket during the Whaling Era. There were still those alive in the far-off Thirties who'd been whaling in the Age of Sail. It was my privilege to sit with them, at Church, at the Town Meetings; to raise my hat to them on the street, and to converse with them at the Restaurant, and in The Leopard. It was my great fortune that they loved to talk, as I loved to listen.

Their recollections and their gossip awakened my curiosity about the old life. I read my way through the extensive collections of the Nantucket Library, on whaling, sailing, the contribution of the industry to world economy, and the collapse of the prosperous Local Economy in the 1880s when kerosene replaced whale oil as the lighting fuel.

The written history was extensive. There was much scholarly work; and, the Library contained, even more to my delight, the Kellogg Collection of seagoing logs and memoirs.

The brief notations in the Logs, the observations of the weather, of the stars, the winds, the currents, all revealed, more than the scholarly histories, the immense, the astounding extent and variety of knowledge necessary for mere survival at sea, let alone that sufficient to navigate the globe, in pursuit of the largest creature ever to live, and to hunt it to death in a small wooden boat, armed only with spears.

Yes, I contracted (or rediscovered) the young boy's love of adventure. And I was there to hear spoken the last tales of the men who'd lived it.

Electricity had replaced kerosene, which replaced whale oil; Bakelite replaced baleen, as the material for corset stays, and the flapper dress abolished the corset; steam had long usurped the place of sail, and, one by one, the last salts of that age went to the graveyard.

One of them had been a mate on the *Thetis, New Bedford*, for three voyages, under sail, in the 1880s.

William Dunne, I believe, enjoyed my company. At the least, I know he loved to "tell the Tale," and he knew I loved to listen.

Pet heard many of them, half-hidden, wide-eyed, in my Beach shack. I recall she asked me, that summer, "Can Captain Dunne's stories be *true*?" I replied, "Many of them, I'm sure."

She nodded and looked thoughtful. "What is it?" I said.

"Papa," she said, "We love the Island."

"Yes," I said, we did.

"We want to know what the Men did."

"Yes," I said, "it was an historic time."

"What did the women do?" she said.

～

I have noted, as, perhaps have you, that the seemingly chance occurrence or comment, when we are in luck, may bring a new insight to a vexing problem, in my case, that summer, the question of co-education.

Her question occupied me all that afternoon. The notes on my desk, sitting undisturbed these last weeks, concerned The Daughters of Zelophead (Numbers 27: 1-11).[61] Dry, academic stuff, I knew,

---

61 These had been balked of their inheritance when their father died in battle. They petitioned Moses for his estate to be divided among them. He responded that such was not the Law, and they asserted that the Law, then, must be changed, and he should lay the matter before the Lord. The Lord ruled in their favor, the Law was changed, and Jewish tradition held that the Bible – The Old Testament – had been written by seven people: Moses, Joshua (after his death), and the five daughters of Zelophead.

more a pompous assertion of my learning than an example of my thought.

But, as Jellicoe said, "When one cannot answer a question, ask a question which admits of an answer."

Pet's question was, "What did the women do?"

This was sufficiently oblique to St. Ives co-education to allow my Id to accept it as provocative, and sufficiently aligned to appease my Schoolmaster ego. So I set myself to find out.

My first, my most important, and certainly my most fascinating information was that of Captain Dunne. I asked him Pet's question that evening at The Leopard (a Nantucket tavern destroyed in the hurricane of 1951).

He put his whisky down, and smiled. "The curious thing," he said, "is that nobody before ever asked."

And then he began to tell me stories of a society split into two parts, male and female, conjoined only for those brief months between the whaling ship's putting in, and pulling out: two or three years at sea, two months at home. "We mixed," he said, "like oil and vinegar, just for that short time, in the greens. The men went back to sea, and the women continued running the Island."

"Glad to see him come, thrilled to see him leave," was the catchphrase of the day. For the women had their island to run, the children to raise, and their own domestic adventures, follies, and tragedies to pursue.

For the Island, in those days, was, as Captain Dunne said (as, of course, it must have been), "a second Lesbos; none of our business, and one wouldn't ask—as neither would the women of life on shipboard, in this or that Port, or in The South Seas. That was the way it was."

[I later discovered several references to the phenomenon of the New England Matriarchies; the sections dealing with sexuality in (generally not very good) Greek—Latin, I suspect, being thought too accessible to the laity.]

There appeared, some years after this time, the excellent "Seven Sisters and the Matriarchy of New England Female Education," by Dr. Marion Hinton Gair (1954), which offered, long past my tenure on the co-education committee, fresh insight and wisdom I could well have used at the time.

In any case, the question on the floor, as put by Pet, was, "What did the women do?" and the answer was, "They ran the town." No man of sense has ever questioned the administrative abilities of women. Though men, in solidarity, may jibe or chaff, we all know who runs the household; and, in honesty, realize that the administration of any larger body cannot, finally, be very much different, nor require more finesse, wisdom and patience (and misdirection) than that which the good wife employs at the kitchen table.

But that was not the question before me that summer.

Are women more educable than men? Girls are certainly more educable than boys, a fact of which only the childless are unaware. It was that observation which led me to the question's answer.

Girls learn differently than boys. They are—if not genetically, then culturally—more likely to sit and listen; they mature more quickly than boys physically, and the onset of puberty, sexual maturity, and nubility inspire a necessarily earlier understanding of the world's dangers and, so, of self-restraint. They, thus, require, at school age, protection where the young boy requires control. I understand (or I believe I understand) something of the needs of boys, I was once one myself.

As Head, my responsibility was not to provide equality of education, but to provide education for boys. I was neither tasked, nor, I saw, was I *fitted* to do so for girls (I lacked the experience and the understanding); further, I was fitted *even less* to adjudicate *between* the sexes, their various and often conflicting needs, *and their nascent or indeed vehement sexuality.*

My answer to Pet's question about Nantucket was, "Whatever the women did, it seems they did well," and that was the answer I took back to the Committee: St. Ives, in my opinion, should remain a school for Boys. I would advise the Committee to class co-education with those other notions, beloved by those thinking themselves discoverers of Novelty, the eventual implementation of which are usually both unfortunate and inevitable.[62]

~

Robison, at Treviss and Hilton, responded to Hollis's rage over the "high-handed defacement of my book."

Below are the surviving pages of Hollis's reply:[63]

And it occurs to me that the Emersonian Transcendentalism—a hodgepodge of good-will, good-intentions, and the attitudes potentially derived therefrom (see also the exuberant muddle of Walt Whitman, who, absent either talent or the ability to recognize it, extemporized a transcendental moan, or happy dirge, in which the recognition that "everything is one," replaces the traditional requirements for rhyme, rhythm, and meaning).

---

62 EDITOR'S NOTE: The Racial Integration of the School in 1960 bears its own testimony (both to those who consider it laudable, and to those who hold it came too late). Hollis, himself (Letter to Whittaker, Yale), cites what he describes as his "dilatoriness," as "particularly indictable"; as "both I and the School spring from the Unitarian and Episcopal New England seeds of Abolition. I cannot excuse my tardiness save by noting that those actually capable of recognizing what is right independent of and prior to the opinion of the World are Prophets. I am not one."

63 Never sent, but found in his workbook of 1965. Ed.

As in the High, so, always, in the Low. For we find the contagion of muddy thought, taken up for gain by the snake-oil salesman of the Agora. I refer to the "self-help" movements which were the grasping step-children of transcendentalism.

See the magic phrase of Émile Coué,[64] "every day in every way I am getting Better and Better"; the populist-mystic writings of Elbert Hubbard, "the supreme prayer of my heart is . . . simply to be radiant" (what can that mean?); the late-appearing applied do-gooderism of Dale Carnegie, "How to win friends and influence people" (1936), which, it seems, improved on Hubbard, in suggesting that they merely "appear" radiant; and its full-out and unabashed financial work-book, the positive mental attitude of Napoleon Hill's *Think and Grow Rich* (1937).

But whether all is within one, an illusion, or with the gods; whether All is Everything, Everything is One, or Everything is Nothing, we must still put food in the larder.

Many a productive man is a misanthrope, and many a fine intellect is possessed by a depressive. Great intelligence and intuition in Women of a depressive proclivity often turns to neurasthenia through want of outlet; as it does, indeed, in men.

Should women be educated? Women are human beings. You question my entry on co-education, as potentially inspiring the cry of "misogyny." Would you have feared the same, had I suggested different categories for men and women in sports? My concern is with human thought and the possibility of its employment in learning. I will specifically address your implication that I consider women inferior in thought.

"Thinking," does not solve all things. We are in fact challenged to say what "thinking" is—and how it differs from both instinct and emotion. But we know this: that it is *effort*, and, as

64 c. (1901–1920. Ed.)

such, its expenditure leads to depletion, continuation in the face of which may progress to various psychological ills, fatigue the least of these.

Are these worse among women? They may, perhaps, be more apparent as (in my experience) woman are more rational than men, and generally more capable of self-restraint—lapses, then being more apparent.

I have never seen great intellect without that fatigue (at the least) which comes from its constant employment (such *always* exacerbated by want of outlet); nor great wisdom without sadness. Absent expression, how can intellect and wisdom but progress from these chronic concomitants to the more acute traumas— the mind and spirit, unused, turning on themselves? Where else would they turn?

I am not unacquainted with the specter of a fine mind locked in madness. You are, I believe, aware of (DEFACED BY HOLLIS'S OWN HAND), and one other case in my family. Both of these women were beloved by me.

I always attributed the severity of their maladies to the lack of education, and, thus, of its outlet in practice of a profession. The notion that I oppose education for women is unsupportable, as is your suggestion that the inclusion of the essay represents that view.

To assert A) is not to unsay B).[65]

---

65 There was no conclusion nor signature, but the penciled inscription "an angry letter, actually unsent." Ed.

RELIGIOUS TOLERANCE

The Five Brothers have always had religious affiliations with the Protestant Faith.

Various waves of traditionalism and innovation (this called a return to First Principles) have succeeded each other in our schools, a healthy or wary patience with their progress contributing to their survival as Religiously Affiliated Institutions.

Jellicoe's slight preference for those in Holy Orders was always attributed to that profound Abolitionism inspired by the Second Great Awakening, and his allied reverence for the Chaplains of his acquaintance in the Union Army.

These, of course, were much more largely Baptist, Methodist, and Catholic than Anglican, which last profession was the more likely to be represented among those who had purchased a Surrogate.

But he was of the Episcopal Religion, a Man of Faith, and, a founder of the School, and disposed to award its Chaplaincies of course, and Masterships and Proctorhoods to his fellow Communicants.

He was a man of Religion, which, to any other than the Epicurean, would, in his day, mean "Religion As I Know It, that is, *true* religion."

"Religious toleration is all very well," he wrote (Postwar Diaries). "But we might take care not to confound our good manners and paternalism. For though the More Established Faiths may congratulate ourselves upon the presence, in our midst or, occasionally, at our tables, of those whom good manners forbid us from openly characterizing as 'the Heathen' the reverse is not true. We do not find among the Baptists or Methodists, our Brothers in Christ, the urge to garner their celebrations by display of a Unitarian."

Fossett's brother, Gerald (Fr. Gerald Fossett, S.J.) was the first Catholic to take the pulpit at Chapel. This was during the intensely anti-Catholic feeling, universal in the South, and growing in the Industrial North.

I was in Hospital in London and I learned of this enormity of Ecumenicism by a letter which, for all its well-bred outrage, could not disguise what I took to be a school-wide (if grudging) admiration for the Priest's courage.

We of the less-stringent Faiths cannot escape an awe at the actual practice of self-abnegation. We may call our confusion sexual curiosity, or dismiss it, with contempt as pointless folly, but it can never be totally expunged. I believe we are stunned by instances of actual self-control. It shames our sophistries, and reveals our pretensions as cant.

During my Tenure as Head the Board mooted the possibility of severing our connection with the Episcopal Church. This was presented by the newly enlightened as a rational modernism. The Meeting of October, 1935, had put the resolution upon the agenda.

I came with a friend. When it was my turn, as it fell out, to address the various proposed benefits of change, I agreed, that, perhaps, the time had, indeed come, and introduced the friend who would, with their permission, address the Board in my stead.

He was Monsignor Francis Sullivan, of the Catholic Archdiocese of Boston.

He welcomed the opportunity to address his fellow Christians, and brought Greetings from His Eminence the Archbishop, offering to create, for us, at our simple request, the Roman Catholic Parish of St. Ives, with all appurtenant privileges, including the appointment not only of a Chaplain-Confessor, but of any number of Priests as Teachers, their salaries and subsistence to be paid by the Archdiocese.

I'd met Frank Sullivan in France, where he, prior to taking Orders, was a Lieutenant in the Princess Pats, on our Left at Loos. After the Board meeting we repaired to Locke-Obers, as was our usual practice, but he would not hear of me picking up the check, for he said it was the most fun he'd had since Repeal.

A SIMILAR INSTANCE[66]

A dedicated Historian of the School, an Old Boy, asked me about the absence in the book of the "story of Brandt." I was surprised that it was known at all, outside the number of the Board convened at that long-ago date.

I believe the Old Boy had gained his knowledge from membership in a group concerned not with the School, but with another aspect of identity. In any case, I add the story here.

Brandt had formed an acquaintance with a railroad porter, one Eugene Starr.

Starr was the grandson of Slaves. His father, James, a blacksmith, had moved from Mississippi to Chicago during Reconstruction. There he was employed in a hardware store in that capacity, and in the (then) allied trade of locksmith, which he taught himself.

Eugene Starr was educated in the Public Schools, and raised to the trade, in the hardware store. This was located adjacent to the Union Stockyards, and was the preferred emporium of the Union Cowboys, those drovers who accompanied the herds, shipped by rail, from The West.

The cowboys came to rely on the blacksmith for the repair and manufacture of those various and eccentric metal accoutrements specific to their trade: horse furniture, farrier instruments, belt buckles, rough gunsmithing, and so on.

---

66 Written for inclusion in the book's Second Edition (never completed), and discovered in Hollis's files by the Editor.

The Backroom of the store, the forge, became the Rialto of the Union Cowboys. Here the boy was raised not only in the trades of his father, but amid the camaraderie of trail hands—in the tales of Indian Fights, Stampede, buffalo hunts, rough mischief in the Trail Towns, and sufficient danger to turn the head of any boy.

Eugene Starr begged his father, and one summer was finally allowed to accompany a cowhand back to Texas, where he made the last cattle drive up the Chisolm Trail (1889).

His cowhand mentor, like Starr, was a colored man, as were some quarter or fifth of the profession; and as were all of that day's railway porters. It was there, in the train's "bunkhouse" on the return trip, that our friend found a second romance, which would lead to his subsequent profession, and a life of travel serving not only the Line and its passengers, but his Community.

For the Porters were, then as now, the Travelling Heralds of the Black Race—bringing and receiving news from around the country to its clearinghouse in Chicago.

The young boy became an unofficial Mascot of the Porters of the Line. Brandt always spoke with wonder and admitted envy of the life of his friend on the Rails, absorbing the lessons and lore of the most exotic and ever-expanding group of preceptors, recipient of the most thorough course in anthropology ever devised: the study (in that anonymity of the servant) of the passengers.

The wealthy, the great, and the notorious were his lesson plan. The young boy was doubly constrained—by his profession and race—to be Seen, not Heard. "And seldom seen at that."

Brandt compared his friend's apprenticeship to that of the Spartans, whose school was the Palaestra.

Starr told how he'd brought a breakfast tray, one morning, to the compartment of Harry Houdini, who was working out a Puzzle Effect—a gift for his son.

Houdini separated the impossibly entwined metal pieces, and, rejoining them, challenged the boy to do the same. He, of course, was assured of the boy's failure, but experienced consternation and surprise at the Starr's duplication of the effect.

This lead to Eugene's employment, for two years, as backstage assistant for Houdini's 1895-96 European tour.

~

Brandt, teaching in that period when the Head and the Masters were expected to cultivate idiosyncrasy was, if not admired, tolerated as an Amateur Magician.

He was travelling in (DATE ILLEGIBLE) back from the Denver meeting of the newly-formed Association of Private Schools.

In his compartment practicing sleights with cards, he pressed the porter into service as audience, asking him to "pick a card, any card."

Brandt could not complete the trick, as the selected card, when he searched for it, had somehow vanished from the deck. He apologized to the Porter, and confessed he could not find the card. Starr said, "it is in your right-hand pocket," as, indeed, it was. And that was the beginning of his friendship with the man Brandt called "the most completely educated person I have ever known."

Brandt spoke of Starr often to his classes. He was upbraided on several occasions, when an inspired boy "kicked over the traces" and ran off to sea, or joined the Marines, or the circus.

Chastised not only for "incitement to riot," but for putting the boys in danger, he responded that the greater danger was preparation for a life empty of both adventure and wonder. He was reminded that, be that as it may, the school existed as a paying institution, and if half the boys ran off, it could no longer afford to pay the teachers, nor, thus, to instruct the staid remainder.

He was also criticized by the reminder that he himself was *not* the world's Most Romantic Railway Porter, but a teacher of mathematics. I was a young teacher, newly raised to Assistant Head, at a meeting of the Board, and so witnessed his humiliation there, capped by that closing gibe.

I have never seen a man so wounded by a thoughtless comment. He was devastated, not by the suggestion that he was a "mere instructor of mathematics," a position of which he was proud, but that his superiors found it good to mock his friendship with a great teacher. I was saddened indeed to hear of his resignation. I pleaded with him to stay, but he would not.

FROM JACKSON'S DISSENT
IN KOREMATSU

"There are those who will jigger the system to insure that the guilty suffer; and those who will employ its inconsistencies to the last degree to insure that they go free. How is the line found between the two, the first invoking the purpose, the second the form, of the Law?

"We empanel twelve persons of diverse intelligence, present a drama, the two positions impersonated by actors called Advocates, and poll the audience.

"Under what circumstances can this process produce Justice? Only if Justice is the name of the process, rather than the result.

"A just result could, as easily, be arrived at by the casting of lots, here substituting Chance for debate. And, perhaps this is the reason for the Jury System's longevity: that it is an assertion of the human *inability* to act with justice, either in the street or in the Court—that is, finally, however it is denied, *is* trial-by-ordeal, or the casting of lots: the possibility of reasoned Justice, here, being found equal *but not connected to* that of unanimity of opinion in a random audience judging between two mountebanks."

～

Hollis wrote to Jackson, whom he had known as a Fourth Former:

The Trout in the Milk, is of course, racism.

I perceive your nicety in finessing the question, for, in our late day, accusing anyone of Racial Prejudice can only occasion rage. Most especially when, as in this case, the accusation's completely warranted.

How odd the Nazis accorded to the Japanese the status of Honorary Aryans, but that Roosevelt could not.

We are, as you know, planning the admittance of Negroes to the School.

It will happen, but with what speed I cannot say, given the current composition of The Board.

—Hollis to Jackson, May, 1944

STORY OF A BAD BOY

In my school days all of us read Thomas Baily Aldritch's *The Story of a Bad Boy* (1869).

His crimes would, today, be considered only pranks. (If boys today commit pranks. I am inclined to think they do not.)

A prank, of course, is mischief committed with no intent to wound. It is, or was, the culturally permitted (I might say tacitly encouraged) discharge of that urge to individuation which, in the late adolescent, contains and must contain some performance of opposition.

School-against-school, or House-against-House rivalries reveal the permitted nature of these performances. I note the abduction of rival team mascots (See: The Bull in the Common Room, *The Misfit*, Fall, 1935). My favorite was the dismantling and reassembly in the Head's anteroom (then my own) of a Packard Roadster.

Breaking bounds, smoking on the sly, and the occasional presence on campus of spirituous liquors (I will not say the smuggling into the Dorms persons of the opposite sex. Though I have heard of it, I can not credit it); these might join The Prank under the head of that mischief of which one must say, "boys will be boys."

As, of course, they will. Their exemption under that head, will not extend to vandalism and misdemeanors verging upon crime. (Theft, malicious mischief, physical abuse, and so on.) But these last were seldom seen by me at School. This does not mean they did not occur. For certainly the position of Teacher, Master, Head, decreasing contact with the boys as they increase bureaucratic responsibilities, might result in an unwarranted sanguinity. But, on the whole, I've been most pleased with the standard of our boys' correct behavior, and of the operational of institutional wisdom in channeling their naturally occurring energies (and anxieties) into safe channels.

I do not think I am a "Pollyanna," but I know that absent sports, clubs, dramatic entertainments, and, indeed, pranks, the adolescent's energies must fall under the direction of unlicensed leaders, and these are more likely than traditional models to lure and lead the young into obscenity, error, and those debaucheries (drinking, narcotics, gambling, and seduction) which, if they are not discovered and corrected, must progress from immorality to outright crime.

Things must be forbidden to boys (as they are to us all) so they will learn what the Law is, and to what extent it may be taunted, and to what it must be obeyed; and, most importantly, who will pay the price for the determination.

My "old fashioned" views, as above, have always been well known. In my early teaching days I was exempted from derision because of my service in France; my notions of discipline, then, respected by the Boys as those of a soldier, rather than an "old schoolmarm." (Though, in effect, they were fairly identical.)

I have seen four or five generations of teachers and parents enthralled by "new ideas in education," each revealed, after no great lag, as foolish or pointless—the confabulation of "educators," whatever *they* may be.

I have always thought of them as brothers to the "consulting Fireman." The house is burning, and one, eager to get the best possible advice, writes to the most notable consultant: "Dear Sir: Flames are consuming my house, what should I do? Your prompt response will be appreciated."

For the education of the boy is happening constantly. Time cannot be turned back, and the lessons avoided, or mislearned on

Tuesday, are embedded in and limiting the mind as a turned ankle restricts the movement and, so, development of the body.

To gain and keep the attention and trust of the young is the first requirement of education. That done, much can be accomplished for their benefit; without that, *less* than nothing, for without that they are being taught contempt.

Easily said. But one must have goals.

My views being well known, I was often asked this: "Have you never met a Bad Boy?" (The question asked with greater frequency after the release of the film *Boys Town* (1938), and Father Flannagan's assertion of the contrary.)

Have I met a Bad Boy?

There is a point at which charity and mercy to the offender is injustice to the mass. I have had a school to run, to accomplish which order must be preserved.

The current fad to construct "Student Governments," and, I have heard, to invite students to sit on the School Board, is foolishness, encouraging the young to, correctly, indict their elders of either hypocrisy—if, as must be clear, final and important decisions must be made by mature authority—or insanity, in awarding to the young an equal voice with their preceptors. (Does the family poll all members and decide important questions by Majority Rule? How terrifying for the children to be thus *cruelly* abandoned in the name of Democracy.)

There have been cases where a boy was dismissed. I have felt, and believe it is still an institutional sentiment, to find such a failure on the part of the school. But institutions, and individuals, do fail.

∾

A young teacher came to Jellicoe for forgiveness or punishment after some (real or imagined) lapse in his duties.

"I failed today," he said. And Jellicoe replied, "Don't tell me that you failed today. You failed one thousand times today."[67] As do we all. Our power is so great, and the importance of example, to the boy, *paramount* in his formation.

I've counseled teachers that sometimes one, having exhausted his abilities, energies, and it may be, good nature, to no effect, must say, "perhaps the wisdom of it will be revealed to me on some later day."

Boys are human beings. As such, they are the possessors of randomly distributed attributes, abilities, and, indeed, deficiencies. My experiences in the Trenches broke me from a mindless, Emersonian understanding of Human Nature as good. It is not good, though *acts* may be good; and men, judged on the balance of their acts, may be called good. An honest assessment of the infrequency of the appearance of these acts and men will tell its own tale.

And some men are (by training, disposition, or genetically) devoid of conscience. These we may call incorrigible, or sociopathic, or any number of useful terms meaning "I can neither understand, nor amend it. Neither can we live with it in our midst."

It is arrogance to assume anyone possessed of skill and understanding sufficient to overcall all difficulties. The surgeon and the lawyer encounter cases for which their expertise cannot prevail. So it is with the teacher. One cannot learn trigonometry in ignorance of arithmetic, nor deportment and cooperation absent that human desire for community called conscience. The alienists, psychiatrists, psychologists, and criminologists may name this absence and be paid for so-doing, much as both the medical and legal professions are paid for failed efforts of their own.

---

67 Jellicoe was regularly complimented on his axiom, and always took care to note it not his own. The source of the quotation has not been found.

But the labeling of the aberrant (largely a matter of fashion) does nothing either to aid the sufferer—if they indeed suffer—nor those upon whom he entails grief.

It was the duty of our State's Governor (two of whom were Old Boys) to approve the sentence of Death upon the condemned. As it was my duty, in France, to affirm the verdict of several Courts-Martial.

It was my duty, also, to report to the Police a boy whom I suspected, and was found to be, the perpetrator of two heinous crimes in the vicinity of school. Rereading my note for the above, I find the verb, in my original, was "denounce."

The schoolmaster's illusion of and fear of omnipotence are aligned. Finally, it is good to be conscious of one's responsibilities, and to question one's motives—even of reflection.[68]

---

68 Those interested in the crime, may find it through reference to the Boston papers of May and June, 1928. The story is widely held to have been the inspiration for Frank Whitton's novel.

A MODEST PROPOSAL: ON MY RETIREMENT FROM TEACHING

I do not know what is meant by the study of English Literature, save that it consists of memorizing and repeating middle-brow platitudes about some author's work.

These, if uttered in polite conversation, would get one branded as a boor. But in schools they are graded, and grades assigned, for choice, to those whose writing holds the least life, or displays the least resistance to "instruction."

What would be said, of any boy, who wrote that Emerson is a pompous fraud, that Whitman a poseur, that Fenimore Cooper is unreadable, and that we've never produced a poet worthy of the name?

How would any boy have accrued such wisdom, or the strength of character to've formed his own opinions, and expressed them, on request, knowing their expression might bring many things but these would not include advancement or approbation?

Yes, yes, there are those who increase our knowledge and enjoyment by annotating Boswell, or Pepys, and we must call them scholars. But who are the rest? And what can be said of a man who trots out, every Fall Term for twenty years, his same notes on Thoreau?

His case is like that of the famous Dr. _____, at Massachusetts General.

He, in the 1880s, was famed for his uncanny ability to diagnose typhoid. He would walk the wards, his students spellbound, and point to a far bed and proclaim, "that man has typhoid. Go over and see if you can determine how I have arrived at my diagnosis."

The students would examine the charts, take the man's vital signs, interrogate him, and, yet, be unable to confirm the diagnosis. Dr. ____ would watch, look in the man's mouth, thump his chest, and announce that in three to five days, the early symptoms of the disease would make themselves known. As, indeed, they would, for Dr. ____ was a carrier.

As are these supposed Educators, who infect an ever-renewed crop of victims with their noxious cant.

What can one say about a book? That it is good or bad? Does not each reader have the right to arrive at his own opinion? If not, would he be inclined (if not actually required) to enjoy a bad book authenticated as good? Or to discard one he enjoyed because it had been shunned by Authority? This latter case is most to the point. For consider those productions banned, as a matter of taste or of morality, but dear to the boys for whom they were written.

In my youth, they were still called "dime novels." Today[69] they are called comic books. They are a step below (and, so, more enjoyable than) the semi-approved Boy's Fiction of G. A. Henty, P. C. Wren, the *Boy's Own Paper*, and so on. They are regarded by Academia as trash and, so, beneath notice, save that which plumps for their censorship or elimination.

It is low wit to suggest we invert the prohibition, disparaging Hawthorne, and requiring the study of Captain America. No doubt this inversion will, one day, take place, but it will not encourage the study of literature.

As for teaching the boys to write, any survey of that called literature will convince that few can write, and, of those few, fewer write well. It is ubiquitous nonsense that the study of writing teaches a

---

69 1958. Ed.

man to organize his thoughts. How can it be so if authority rewards him only for reporting the thoughts of others?

There is much merit in that clarity necessary for writing a letter of business; and, indeed, much of the actual literature of our Twentieth Century seems to share that forthrightness of a dunning letter. But neither the remorseless resolve of the businessman nor that of the novelist can be learned in school.

Most of that passing as literature must be classed with the love letters. The recipient, if moved at all, is likely moved by the display in the writer of perseverance against impossible odds; the noble struggle here that to force compliance, not from the obdurate heart, but from the uncaring English Language.

AFTERWORD

by George Choate

It was my great pleasure to have known Mr. Hollis (The Head; for three generations of boys).

I was a Sixth Former (Twelfth Grade) at The School during his last years as Headmaster.

He would often sit in on Carleton Brewster's lectures on English Poetry, unobtrusive, at the back of the room. He had that quality, rare among the greatly celebrated, of actually becoming part of a group.

He sat, as would another student, his focus directed (sadly, more than ours) upon the speaker, and set upon the day's topic.

He seemed to have that quality of curiosity, not to say wonder, possessed by the very young boy, and, how often, sadly, eradicated by schooling.

I recall my classmate (I name him with his permission), Austin Sherman, raising his hand during the lecture on The Lake Poets and asking, "What is so interesting about a *Lake*?" (Judge Sherman, to his credit, was not being impertinent, but merely unprepared. A habit he did not take with him into his chosen profession.)

The class laughed, the lecture continued, Sherman was not abashed, but confused. Mr. Hollis saw it, and beckoned him, at the end of class.

"Mr. Sherman," he said, "that is a good question. Well and simply put. Socrates would have honored you, as I must. When we cannot reduce the most daunting and intricate of problems to simple inquiries; when we 'philosophize,' and use large words to hide from ourselves our ignorance, we squander that sole property which distinguishes us from the Beasts. You had a legitimate question, you asked it with courage. That it may have arisen from lack of preparation is another thing. But better confession of ignorance in the quest for knowledge, than rote repetition of a received, unquestioned proposition."

Sherman beamed his thanks. He began to walk away.

"One thing," Hollis said, "Should you read them, you will find the 'Lake' of the Lake Poets refers not to their subject, but to their situation. Their *subject* was erotic love."

The closing comment could have been made by any teacher trying to lure a boy to a subject. The previous one only by a great teacher, sharing his love of knowledge with a precious, unformed mind.

I remembered the incident, as who would not, and brought it up in conversation with The Head, during my return to The School for some Reunion.

He was in retirement, alone, after the death of his wife (1966), and cared for (though he needed little care, being, until his death, vigorous) by Mrs. Wade. His comfort was overseen at a respectful distance by the Trustees and the informal Old Boys network; and he was more put upon to reject assistance than to request it.

In any case, I recalled to him his comment to Sherman. He shook his head sadly. "I have always regretted it," he said. I asked him why.

"Because the mention of erotic love was cheap," he said.

"As it was about Sex?" I asked.

"Not at all," he said. "Not at all. But it was *superfluous* to my major promise, and, so inelegant. I always wished it unsaid."

His regrets, and he had many, were, it seems, usually on that order: an extra word spoken, the inability to withhold comment, an ambiguous direction given; these were the regrets of an Infantry

Officer, which he had been (Captain, Brevetted Major, Welsh Guards).

I suggested to him that his "style" with the boys, was that of the good Company Commander. He smiled at the compliment, and said, "Ah, perhaps."

~

He was an orphan, raised on his parents' death, as "the poor step-child," in his sister's husband's home in Medford, Massachusetts.

His stepfather, Herbert Clare, was "a small businessman with a large family," and happy, it seems, to vent his various frustrations on the cuckoo chick. "I, for my part in the proceedings, was always obligingly failing."[70]

He had been put back twice, in the Medford Public Schools.

Shamed, he had run away, at age twelve, "the perpetual resident of the third grade."

He was found in New York City, living in the Park. The Child Welfare Board returned him to Medford, where he was beaten by his stepfather, Clare; an occurrence which was not unique.

He ran away again, at age thirteen, to Portland, Maine. There he tried to sign on to a sailing ship as cabin boy or deckhand. The port authorities contacted Mrs. Clare, who came to retrieve him.

He told her no force on earth would return him to that house, and she said she agreed with his decision. Her lifelong friend, Prudence Voll (then Mrs. Samuel Worth, of Boston), appealed, through her husband, Worth (an Old Boy, St. Ives '72), to Jellicoe.

"This is a thoroughly bad boy," Worth had written; "he is a sullen truant, and apparently ineducable. You will love him."

---

70 Charles Hollis, Private Correspondence, courtesy of Sir Andrew Ross-Merry, letter dated February 12, 1938.

As, indeed, Jellicoe did. And the boy flourished, under him and under Fossett.

I asked Mr. Hollis if he harbored resentment, not to say, rage, over those who had mistreated and misunderstood him as a boy.

"Not at all," he said, "I am indebted to them for the most precious of gifts."

"What was that?" I asked.

"A bad example," he said.

We see, in his "Informal Remarks," to the twentieth reunion of the Class of '14 (his class):

I have found, as I am sure you have, too, that exemplars of virtue are rare. Indeed, we know it, who consider ourselves, *in the main* virtuous, but find our own instances of real courage or restraint rare; as rare, in fact as those the lack of which we so rightly decry in others.

Many of you served in the War. There, you will recall, we were taught Land Navigation.[71]

There, I found, the most useful of tools was "Back Bearings." When we were uncertain of our course *to* the desired destination when we lacked a terrain feature or visual waypoint, we could always turn and determine our previous course, and, turning the compass, simple extend it forward.

Back bearings, similarly, and I hope you will excuse the nicety of the conceit, can be taken in life, gauging not behavior of *others*, as a course from which we must digress, but behavior of our *own*, perceiving, in honest assessment of its course, a destination, the desirability of which goal we may wish to reconsider.

---

71 It was his habit to overlook service in the Navy as a courteous dismissal of a gaffe. Mine included. This, when brought to his attention, he apologetically amended, for the short time he held it in memory.

The school, during his Headmastership, and, under his influence, until his death, had no standardized criteria for admission—all applicants being invited to submit an application and visit, when "the suitability of the School for their needs" (Jellicoe's words), might be determined.

Asked what he looked for in a potential student, he always replied, in Jellicoe's words, "give me the ne'er-do-wells." (He, of course, was one. I, perhaps, another.)

This was the Motto of the Humor Magazine—featured under its masthead, in every issue—from which it took its name, *The Misfit*.

∾

I am privileged to have been selected by the Board (the Literary Executors of his Estate), to edit these papers.

"Old men forget, and all shall be forgot." The fame of even Ozymandias must disappear, as will that of the poet who sung of the process.

Charles Hollis is honored by his former students, still, as a memory. Among the current boys he is, at best, a Legend, which soon will be a myth, and then not even that.

St. Ives will change, as it has changed, as all things change, "the good, sometimes changed into the better—but, eventually, into their opposite." "The urge to preserve and the urge to improve are equally profitless, *sub specie aeterinitatis*." "In the moment, and in every moment, however, there is, however remote, the possibility of virtue." Charles Hollis (1938).

—George Choate, Nantucket, 2022